ORPHAN TRAIN TRAGEDY

RACHEL WESSON

CHAPTER 1

NEW YORK, APRIL 1904

athleen Green looked furtively around her as she walked down the street, toward the tenement building. The biting wind chilled her to the bone as she drew her coat closed. She passed dirty children dressed in threadbare clothes. Dressed being an overstatement as in some cases, the children wore little more than a rag to cover their dignity. She didn't fear these children, they were too young. She wanted to stop and share the contents of her basket, but there were too many. If she gave food to one, she would be overwhelmed and could cause a riot.

The older ones, the ones who had fallen into gangs were another story. They would knock her down and steal her basket without a second's thought. She didn't blame them either. She knew what it was like to go to bed hungry, to endure belly aches so severe they would make a grown man cry. Closing her eyes, she could

1

picture her sisters, Maura and Bridget trying to keep a fire going with newspapers. They didn't have the money for coal and newspapers were often discarded. They didn't produce a long-lasting heat as they flared up and out the chimney.

She kept a firm grip on her basket picking her way through the discarded litter. The early frost was gone leaving a pile of slush in its wake. Children passed her staring at the ground. She assumes they are collecting cigarette ends probably in the hope of harvesting the remaining tobacco and selling it to those who rolled their own cigarettes. The more enterprising would buy a packet of cigarette papers and roll them to sell on as individual cigarettes. Those in more desperate need of money would find other things to sell. She shut her mind off to the route her thoughts were taking.

If Lily knew she was visiting this place without Mini Mike or Tommy to look out for her, she would have a fit. But Kathleen didn't want anyone questioning why she was visiting Granny Belbin, or worse offering to accompany her.

As she walked, her mind drifted back to the days when she'd lived here. If it hadn't been for her sister, Bridget, and Lily, where would she be now?

Kathleen Green, you need to get a grip on yourself. She should be counting her blessings, not looking for trouble. Maybe she should go back to the sanctuary. What she was doing was silly.

"Morning, Kathleen, you look grand."

Kathleen started. She hadn't seen Colm Fleming coming toward her. He was married now with his own family.

"Morning, Colm, how's your family? And your dad?"

"Dad and the family are grand. Mary is expecting again. I told her no more, but she sure loves having a baby in the house."

Kathleen steeled her expression, not wanting her old friend to get a hint of her distress at the mention of babies. He looked uncomfortable.

"Where are you off to? You shouldn't be wandering these streets on your own. Why didn't Tommy or Mike come with you?"

"They were busy, Colm. Don't worry, I won't be stopping long. I have a letter for Granny Belbin from Kenny."

"By the smell coming from that basket, you seem to have brought her some treats too."

Kathleen caught the glimpse of hunger in his eyes.

"Cook just gets better at baking. Want to try some."

"No, I couldn't," Colm said. "You keep it for Granny."

"Colm, you know she won't eat it all but will give it to her birds and whatever other animals she is tending this week. Take a small bit. Hold the basket for me, please."

Kathleen took two cookies and put them in a

3

napkin. She gave the parcel to Colm and took back her basket.

"Thanks Kathleen. I will have a grand breakfast. I best get on my way. I'm on afternoon shift. Be careful, mind how you go."

"You too, Colm. And good luck with the new baby."

Kathleen continued walking, wondering how her old friend would feed his growing family. She would speak to Lily about getting a parcel of clothes and other goodies sent over to his wife. What Colm needed was someone like his mother. When Mrs. Fleming had been alive, she had helped save many in the tenements including Kathleen and her family.

She strode through a small alley before coming to Granny's front door. Taking a deep breath, she knocked. Granny Belbin took her time to answer. She was getting less steady on her feet but refused to admit she was too old to live alone. She opened the door a fraction, then, seeing Kathleen, she opened it wider to let her enter greeting her with a moan.

"'Tis yourself. I wondered if you had forgotten about me."

Kathleen ignored the cranky tone.

"I brought you some cookies. I thought you might like company."

Granny Belbin raked Kathleen from head to foot. "You got something on your mind. You're here for more than just a visit. Out with it. Is it Kenny?"

Kathleen forced the smile on her face, not wanting to show how nervous she was. Granny could tell what she was thinking. No, that was silly, nobody could read someone's mind. Not even when they had the gift of reading tea leaves. A large fire roared in the chimney, a sign Mini Mike and Tommy were keeping Granny in comfort. Kathleen shivered despite the warmth of the room. She shouldn't be thinking of messing with things she didn't understand.

She didn't realize she'd stayed silent so long until Granny spoke again.

"Are you going to stand there like a mute or start talking?"

"Granny, Kenny is fine. In fact, he wrote to you again. I brought his letter. I would love to hear how he is." Kathleen knew Granny Belbin couldn't read anymore. Nobody knew if she ever could but now, she blamed her eyesight. But God help anyone who mentioned her lack of ability. The woman was likely to show the person the door in due speed.

"Suit yerself. I suppose you want a cup of tea too."

Kathleen nodded her head, took off her coat and hung it on the peg on the back of the door.

"Make yerself at home, why don't ya?" Granny muttered.

Kathleen sighed. She was regretting the visit already.

CHAPTER 2

When Kathleen had first come to visit the old woman, she wondered how Lily had the patience to deal with the grumpy old lady. But after all these years, she understood it was anxiety that made Granny the way she was. Life around her was changing. In the old days, she could put the fear of God into the local kids. She'd saved Mini Mike and Tommy from the streets and quite a few others. But now with the likes of Monk Eastman and the other gangs in the area, she didn't feel as protected. Mini Mike and Tommy had put the word out that she was untouchable, but still the old lady fretted. Kathleen wished she would come live at the sanctuary but when Lily offered the invitation, Granny told Lily to leave and take her workhouse with her. Kathleen smiled at the memory of Lily's face when she'd told Kathleen what the woman had said. Lily was so affronted; she didn't care Granny had banned her from visiting. Lily swore she wouldn't come to see the old woman again until her temper settled. But being kind hearted, Lily always made sure Tommy or Mike took a basket of goodies to Granny and checked up on the old woman regularly.

"Will ya start on the letter or is it Christmas you is waiting for?" Granny asked, pulling Kathleen out of her thoughts.

"Sorry." Kathleen opened the envelope in front of Granny to prove she hadn't read it before her visit. She coughed to clear her voice and then started to read.

"*Dear Granny, myself and Jack Jr. are doing fine now. Junior was sad for a while after Jack died, but now he is back to normal. I told him Jack was old and in pain. Ten years is a good age for a dog, don't you think?*"

Kathleen exchanged a smile with Granny before continuing the letter.

"*I hate my new school, but Ma won't listen. I want to be back with Mrs. Collins, but she says I am too old. She says the new master will teach me, as he knows more than she does. I don't think she's right. The new master doesn't seem to know much. He never heard of Hell's Kitchen or Monk Eastman or nothing like that.*"

"Why would anyone need to know about Eastman?" Granny asked, but Kathleen assumed the question was rhetorical. She continued to read.

"*How are you? I hope you are eating properly. Would you come and visit me? Ma says there is plenty*" *of room at our new home. We will take in children from New York. Maybe you could help Ma with them?"*

Granny cackled, interrupting Kathleen. She glanced at the old woman, afraid she was going to choke, but Granny continued to laugh. "Can you imagine me running around a crowd of children? Those days be long gone. Still, what's your sister getting involved with more kids for? I thought she had a weak heart."

Kathleen bristled as she always did when someone spoke disparagingly about her family.

"Her heart is doing much better. Bridget feels the need to care for children and what better way than to take some orphans to live with her?"

Granny didn't react well to her tone.

"There're better ways. Keep them with their families for a start."

"Granny, don't start that again," Kathleen warned. "We don't steal children. We only send real orphans with no family or children whose parents can't keep them."

"Shush. You need not lecture me. I heard it all before. What else does the lad say?"

Kathleen looked back at the letter and continued to read. Kenny sounded like he was having a lot of fun and enjoying Riverside springs. Then she came to the last paragraph.

"Granny, I got a favor to ask ye. Would you put a flower on Mary's grave for her birthday next week? She

always liked flowers. I best go as Ma is calling for me. Love you, Kenny. PS I am coming back to New York in about two years' time. I want to join the Navy and see the world. Ma isn't too happy, but Dad told her she has to let me grow up and make my own decisions. She didn't like that much. She gave him a dirty look, and he told me he was in the doghouse."

Granny sighed, looking out toward the window. Not that she could see anything through the dirt and grime on the glass.

"Young Kenny always had a wanderlust in him. I remember his sister Mary traveling the streets looking for that lad. Always getting in the middle of things. But the Navy? What does he want to go to sea for? He'll get seasick, maybe even drown."

Kathleen didn't want to think about Kenny drowning. She was fond of the boy her sister had adopted.

"Did you make the tea, or would you like me to do it?" Kathleen asked, attempting to distract the woman.

"Keen on having your tea today aren't ya? Do you want me to read the leaves?"

CHAPTER 3

*E*mbarrassed, Kathleen wasn't sure what to say. She didn't believe in the whole reading tea leaves thing. The church frowned on such practices. But what if it could tell her? Nothing else seemed to work. She'd tried touching a rabbit's foot and goodness knew what else. Granny moved restlessly in her seat.

"Do ya or don't ya. I ain't got all day."

Tempted to ask what else was the old woman going to do, Kathleen bit her tongue. There was no point in antagonizing her.

"Sure, go on then. Just this once—only don't tell Father Nelson."

Granny stood up, swaying. Kathleen wanted to help, but she knew she would only be rebuffed. Granny glanced at her.

"Why would I be telling a priest anything?"

"Granny you can pretend with the others, but I know you like Father Nelson. You two have great chats, he told me how interesting your life was."

Granny's forehead creased. Kathleen immediately regretted saying anything, but it was too late.

"He told you about what we talked about?"

"No, Granny, not at all. That's private. He just said he looks forward to seeing you and chatting with you."

Granny bustled about getting cups and saucers and the tea. Then she set it on the table.

"Hmph, he has little to amuse him. Now, come over here and sit down. It's easier for me. Clear that stuff out of your way."

Kathleen did as she was bid. Granny sat down opposite her, stirring the pot before pouring.

"Right, well drink up that cup of tea and let's see what the leaves say."

Kathleen drank the tea, trying not to grimace at the state of the cup. Then she handed it back to Granny who placed it on the table and appeared to study it. She was quiet for so long, Kathleen couldn't bear it.

"What does it say?"

"Kathleen, you can't interrupt and rush things, it takes time. Are ya sure you want to know?"

"Of course," Kathleen replied, hoping she sounded more confident than she felt. Her stomach was churning and the hairs on the back of her neck stood on end. A picture of her mother suddenly darted into her head. She would have given her more than a touch of the wooden spoon for mixing with stuff like this. Filled with doubts, Kathleen stood up.

"Granny I best be going. I forgot..."

"You sit back down and listen to the leaves. You can't just walk out now. Upset the forces, that would."

Kathleen shivered, looking around the room despite herself. This was plain silly. She was a grown woman not a child scared of some bogey man. Granny continued to speak but her voice didn't sound like it was coming from her. It sounded like a young male with a strong New York accent.

"You have a long way to travel. Or maybe someone near to you is going on a trip."

Well, that cleared everything up. Kathleen fumed. She was surrounded by children who went on orphan trains. It wasn't hard to imagine someone leaving.

"You won't have a child of your own if you stay in your marriage. The fault isn't with you."

Kathleen stared at Granny but the woman had her eyes closed. She pinched herself. Was it Richard who couldn't father a child? How could Granny know that? She was about to ask but Granny opened her eyes and started talking again.

"I see a fire. A young girl, helpless and alone. She needs a home."

Kathleen sat forward. "What girl? Where is she? Where are her parents?"

But her questions went unanswered. Granny

continued staring at the cup and speaking in the male voice.

"There is a woman with a black cat. She doesn't like you or your orphans. She means you harm."

Kathleen bit her lip in an effort not to laugh. Granny was really trying to wind her up with her talk of women with black cats. Why didn't she say a witch was going to fly over on her broomstick? Disgusted with herself for even thinking of asking Granny to read the leaves, Kathleen gathered her things together. She was about to stand up when Granny spoke again.

"A foreign boy. He will go with you on the trip. He has a great future ahead of him. But..."

"But?" Kathleen prompted, totally caught up in the moment.

"You must find him the right home. His happiness is in your hands."

Kathleen sat back in her seat. Granny was playing with her. Of course, the children's futures lay with her. Her and the rest of the group working at the sanctuary and the outplacement homes. Granny didn't like them taking children away from New York. This was her way of making Kathleen squirm.

Kathleen went to stand up, but Granny made a sound, and it terrified Kathleen. She glanced at the old woman and was immediately sorry she did for Granny was crossing herself. This from a woman who said she didn't practice her religion any more.

Kathleen's heart raced. "What is it? Tell me."

"Nothing."

Kathleen couldn't let it go, "Granny, I'm a grown woman. I know you saw something. Please tell me." But even as she said the words, she kept thinking of the Bible and how it forbade conjuring up spirits. Father Nelson would be furious.

"See these leaves. They say something bad is coming." Granny held out the cup, her hand shaking. Afraid she would drop it, Kathleen reluctantly took the piece of crockery.

"Like bad weather?" Kathleen's joke didn't amuse Granny. She took the cup away and muttered to herself.

Kathleen didn't want to know anymore. She had to get out of the room.

"Granny, it's late and I best get back to the sanctuary. I have things to sort out before the next orphan train goes out. I will ask Mini Mike or Tommy to come see you soon. Take care."

Granny grabbed Kathleen's arm in a vice-like grip. "Stay away from the water."

"Now you are scaring me. It's not nice."

"I mean it," Granny said, looking serious. "The leaves don't lie. There is something bad, the leaves are at the bottom of the cup. If it were the past, they would rise to the top." Granny stared into Kathleen's eyes, but it was as if she could see right into her thoughts. "I know it's a baby you want. Be careful what you wish for, young Kathleen Collins."

Kathleen didn't bother to correct her name. She wanted to go, out of the dark room for the walls seemed to come in on top of her. She snatched up her hat, muttered goodbye and was out the door before Granny could say another word. She walked as quickly as the hem of her skirt would let her. Why had she gotten involved in something stupid? Hadn't her mam always said it didn't pay to mix with the dark world? She would stop at the church and light a candle. But what if Father Nelson caught her? He'd know she was upset the moment he saw her. She wasn't about to admit to him she had been getting her fortune read.

Kathleen Green, you can be a right eejit.

CHAPTER 4

eddy Doherty waited at the window for his father to come home. He was always late home from work, but today he had promised to come early.

"Teddy, come away from the window. It won't help make Charlie come faster."

"But Mom, he said he would be home early. In time for our birthday party."

His mom pushed her hair from her eyes as she smiled at him.

"Darling, when did your father ever break his promise? Now come and help me set the table."

"That's girl's work. Grace and Evie should do it."

"Theodore Doherty, you mind your manners. Your sisters have their own chores and are not your maidservants. Laurie has already done his bit by collecting the shopping. Now do what I tell you before I send you to bed."

"Mom, you wouldn't do that on my birthday," he whined. "I'm ten today."

Too late, he caught the look his mother exchanged with her friend, Kathleen Green. He liked Kathleen; she was like his aunty but even she looked rather cross today. It wasn't fair. It was his birthday. Everyone should be happy. Kathleen spoke sharply.

"Teddy, ten years old is old enough to know when to admit you are wrong. Off you go now and help your mother."

Kathleen put her hand on his shoulder, rubbing it slightly before pushing him toward the door. He knew it was time to leave and not grumble. But as he closed the door behind him, he couldn't stop himself listening to their conversation.

"Poor Teddy, he's just desperate to get his hands on his presents," his mother said. "That child was born without patience, not like Laurie."

Teddy sighed. Saint Laurie struck again. He loved his twin, he did, but sometimes, occasionally he wished it were his twin who did something wrong. Just for a change.

"Teddy's the image of you, Lily. He can't bear to sit still but has to be on the go all the time. Don't look at me like that. You can't deny it. Five children under the age of ten and you are still working all the hours you can at the sanctuary. Richard worries about you. We all do."

"Kathleen, don't fret for goodness' sake. Hard work killed no one. Charlie is so busy at work these days. Seems to be no end to the corruption his bosses are investigating. Not that you are one to talk, we see more of you now than ever before. Are things all right between you and Richard?"

Teddy moved away from the door. He shouldn't be listening to the adults. He didn't like hearing anyone was worried about his mother. She was his world; he was so proud of what she had achieved. She took him to the sanctuary with her, sometimes. He got to play with the children going on the trains. He was often tempted to slip aboard one of those trains and go on an adventure just like the boys did in the books his father read to him.

Totally forgetting about the table, he went to find Laurie. Maybe his brother would finally get his nose of out his book and go outside to play ball.

He found Laurie with his nose in a newspaper. Tempted to grab the paper out of his twin's hands, he stamped down the impulse.

"Want to go out and play ball?" Teddy asked. "Pa isn't home yet."

"Teddy, read this. The Wright brothers say we will all be able to fly someday. We could take a plane to Europe. Wouldn't that be amazing?"

"Sure." Teddy didn't bother to hide his lack of

interest. What was so wonderful about Europe anyway? Didn't they live in the best country in the world? In the best city. They didn't need to go traveling. If his brother wanted to meet people from Europe, all he had to do was walk down two blocks and meet Germans or Polish people or any other nationality.

He threw himself on the bed, wishing for about the hundredth time he had more brothers. Grace wasn't too bad for a girl. She was quite a good catcher actually. But Evie, she didn't want to do anything but play with dolls. As for Coleen, she just ate and slept. Babies were so dull.

He sighed, causing Laurie to look at him.

"What's up with you?" his brother asked. "Aren't you excited about Dad coming home?"

"Yes, but he isn't here yet."

"He said he would be back by four with a surprise for us. You know Dad. He'll be here. Why don't you do something to pass the time?"

"I want to play ball," Teddy explained. "But I can't do that by myself."

Laurie looked at the newspaper in his hands, then at Teddy, and back to the paper. It was clear he was torn between wanting to please his brother and read about his favorite subject.

"Please Laurence. I already got in trouble with Mom. I can't sit here doing nothing. Save me."

Laurie threw a pillow at him. "After this much

practice getting into trouble, you should be able to save yourself. Come on then. I'm batting."

Teddy whistled. He didn't care if he had to pitch, so long as he was outside.

"Thanks Laurie."

"It's okay. You can pay me back by letting me open my present first." Laurie winked at him to show he was joking. In all their years, Laurie had never opened a present quickly but was content to pull back the paper slowly to reveal what was inside. By the time he found out what he had gotten, Teddy would be playing with his gift.

Teddy clapped Laurie on the back. "You know you're not too awful for a brother."

Laurie seemed to stand taller, but he didn't reply. They were soon in the garden playing and laughing, all worries forgotten.

CHAPTER 5

"They play well together, don't they?" Kathleen stared out the window at the twins.

"They do, despite their differences," Lily agreed. "They are close. Too close, I know Grace feels left out."

"Grace is almost nine. She doesn't know whether to be a child or a little lady. It's an awkward stage. She is a real mother hen too."

"You mean how she looks after the younger children?" Lily asked. "Yes, I'm proud of her. I never knew she was learning German. She seems to have a gift for languages. She wants to be a teacher when she grows up."

Kathleen continued to stare out the window, refusing to look at Lily although she knew of her scrutiny given the pink color in her cheeks.

"Are you going to tell me what's wrong, Kathleen? You know I would never repeat anything. I'm worried about you. You smile and pretend all is right in your world, but your eyes hold a sadness I haven't seen since before you found Shane."

At the mention of her brother, Kathleen smiled slightly, but it didn't remove the sadness. Lily took her arm and led her friend to the sofa where she sat beside her.

"Kathleen, tell me. Please."

Kathleen looked everywhere but at Lily. Lily could feel the shudders running through her friend. Alarmed, she put her arm around Kathleen's shoulders and pulled her close. Something broke inside Kathleen and the tears once they fell didn't stop for some time. Finally, after a deep shudder, Kathleen broke away and rummaged in her purse for a hanky. Lily handed her one of hers.

"It's clean," she promised. "I hope you feel a little better. A cry often does that."

"Look at me, Lily. I'm a mess. A grown-up woman crying like a baby. I don't know what's wrong with me. I have everything I could want. A good husband, Patrick is doing well with school, a wonderful home and amazing friends. I have nothing to cry about."

Lily paused, wondering if now was a good time. She glanced at the clock, but it would be a while before Charlie would be home. The children were occupied.

"Kathleen, why don't you and Richard seek help?"

Kathleen looked shocked and for a second Lily wished she could take back her question. She held Kathleen's gaze, remaining silent.

"For what?"

"I know you have Patrick and he is a wonderful blessing, but you were born to be a mother. You and Richard, well it's been seven years since you got married. Haven't you waited long enough?" Lily hesitated. Kathleen's cheeks were bright red, almost a match for her own. "I don't mean to pry. Maybe you both decided you didn't want a family of your own, aside from Patrick, I mean."

Kathleen shook her head, the tears once more rolling down her cheek. "I love Patrick, I do, but in two years he will be gone. He wants to study at John Hopkins so Richard is doing everything he can to help him get into the school. Then the house will be so empty. Richard works hard. I know his work is valuable, but it means..."

"You are left too much on your own. No wonder you come to the sanctuary so often. Have you spoken to Richard about how you feel?"

Kathleen nodded. She stared toward the unlit fire. "He said, we just need to be patient. He thinks the traumas I faced growing up may have caused some... some problems. I think he is just telling me that. He knows I'm a failure. I can't give him children. He would be better off without me."

"Kathleen Green, you stop that nonsense this minute. You and Richard are a team, a wonderful one. Anyone with eyes in their heads can see your husband is besotted with you."

Kathleen didn't reply but stared past Lily.

"Kathleen, how do you know the problem lies with you? It could just as easily be Richard. He's the doctor. He knows it takes two people to make a baby and if the baby doesn't arrive, it isn't always the woman who has the problem. I think you should seek advice from someone like Doctor Pennington."

"Richard wouldn't like it."

"Richard is a wonderful man, but he is a doctor who specializes in burns. How would he feel if Doctor Pennington tried to treat a burn victim?" Lily could see her point had struck home. "Exactly. Now please tell me you will make an appointment. Maybe Doctor Pennington can help. Maybe he can't, but at least you will know."

"Granny Belbin read my tea leaves," Kathleen said, looking embarrassed.

Lily rolled her eyes. She liked the crusty old woman but had no time for reading tea leaves or Irish leprechauns or rabbits' feet. She thought it was a whole load of nonsense, but she knew the Irish traditionally were a more superstitious group. Although, Kathleen had always seemed so practical to her.

"I know you don't believe in that stuff, but she

caught me on a bad day. One thing led to another..." Kathleen hated lying to Lily, but she just couldn't admit that she had been desperate enough to ask the old woman to read the leaves.

"Kathleen, you don't have to justify yourself. What did Granny say?"

"She saw a child in my future."

"That's good news then, isn't it?" Lily wasn't sure why Granny's prediction hadn't seemed to cheer Kathleen up. Instead, her friend looked even more miserable. "What am I missing? I feel like I am only getting half of the story."

"Granny predicted some other things. She said there would be a young girl on the train who had been involved in a fire. A foreign boy whose happiness depended on me."

"Kathleen, you can read all sorts of things into those predictions. All our orphans depend on us don't they? I think we have had at least one foreign child on each trip, more if you count the Irish."

The joke fell flat.

"Oh, Lily what have I done? I shouldn't be messing with stuff like that. Mam didn't have time for it, at least that's what Bridget says."

"You wrote to Bridget about Granny Belbin?" Lily asked.

"Yes. She told me to forget about the reading and go to see your doctor."

Lily sat back into the sofa. "I knew there was a good reason for me liking Bridget. I wish she was here in New York. How are things going in Riverside Springs?"

"She didn't say much. Said she would get a longer letter in the post soon. Kenny hates school, but what's new about that? He wants to run away to sea, but she's hoping he will change his mind soon. He loves the horses so maybe he will settle down and help his pa out on the ranch. Angel is still teaching; she brings Shane Jr. and Alex into school with her. Bella has her hands full with her three. She said she was feeling better now that Rosie was a little older."

"Did she mention Maura?"

"Not really," Kathleen answered. "She knows I am still looking for her, but she doesn't believe I will ever find out what happened. Maybe she's right. But I won't give up. My brother, Michael, is being released from prison next year, so I still hope to have a family reunion. I guess you think I am soft."

"You are anything but soft," Lily said. "Your family means the world to you and always has. Someday, hopefully, you will get your happily ever after."

A shadow crossed Kathleen's face, along with a terrified expression in her eyes.

"What? What are you not telling me?"

"Granny Belbin said there will be a big tragedy before I get my child. How can I wish for a child if that's the price I have to pay? She said people will die."

Lily pushed down the urge to throttle Granny Belbin. She would have a word with Mini Mike and get him to talk to the old woman. Tell her to stop spreading stories of doom and gloom.

"Kathleen, people die every day. Nobody can predict the future. It's all a lot of old rubbish—fairytales, just like the stories we tell the children. Please, turn on the sensible side of your brain. You never would have taken any notice of tea leaves and all that in years gone by. Wanting a baby so much has made you desperate to believe anything. I am making an appointment for you with Dr. Pennington and that's final. No more Granny Belbin, do you promise me?"

"Yes, Lily."

At her tone, they both exchanged a look and then laughed.

"I feel like Teddy did when you told him off earlier," Kathleen admitted with a smile. "You are rather fierce, Mrs. Doherty."

"Ha! If you think I am fierce you should meet Charlie's Nan. I wish she would come back from Clover Springs for a visit. She hasn't seen the sanctuary since it first opened. But she maintains she is too old to travel." Lily stood up. "Why don't you go upstairs and wash your face and redo your hair? Then you can come and set the table with me."

"I thought Teddy was supposed to do that."

"I love my son, but I know him well. I bet you a dollar that table is as bare as it was an hour ago. But it's his birthday so I will let him get away with it. Just this once."

Kathleen didn't argue. She was fond of Lily's twins but if she had to be honest, Teddy secured a special place in her heart. He was such an adventurous young boy.

CHAPTER 6

*T*he sound of a horn tooting drove them all outside to find Charlie sitting behind the steering wheel of a new automobile.

"Charlie, what are you doing with that horseless carriage?" Lily asked.

"Darling, it's called an automobile, and this is our new mode of transport. They are all the rage. The boss let me borrow it to see if I would like to buy one. He reckons I deserve a treat. Says the law firm has an image to maintain."

Lily couldn't say anything, the look of sheer enjoyment on her husband's face told her he loved it and that was the end of the matter as far as he was concerned. She glanced toward her children and to Kathleen, whose facial expression was a mixture of horror and fascination.

"Papa, you didn't tell us. Can we go for a ride

now?" Laurie hopped from one foot to the other with excitement. Teddy just stared at his father.

"Come on, everyone pile in. Kathleen, you too if you want to risk it. Tie your hat onto your head with a scarf or the wind will blow your hair into your eyes."

Lily and Kathleen grabbed their hats and scarves and sat in the back along with the boys. Grace, Evie and their baby sister stayed behind with Cook. Lily couldn't blame them. She liked to think little scared her, but these machines did. She much preferred a horse and carriage, but she knew automobiles were the way of the future. In time, Charlie would insist she try out the new subway to travel from one side of New York to the other. She shivered, thinking nothing could be worse than voluntarily going underground to sit on a train and traveling so far beneath the earth's surface. She couldn't bear to think of the human cost of making the subway. Less than two years ago, the New York Central Railroad cave in had cost fifteen men their lives and injured dozens of others. The sanctuary had helped where it could by taking in the children until the men recovered and providing food baskets, clothes and medications to the families in need.

The tragedy had particularly affected Charlie. His bosses were still trying to seek compensation for those affected. Her husband had rescued one of his bosses from a train back in the Great Blizzard of 1888. As if reading her mind, Charlie glanced behind him.

"Lily take that look off your face. It's safe. I've had lessons."

She couldn't believe her husband had turned to look at her. "Stop looking at me and keep your eyes on the road."

Kathleen grasped her hand and Lily kept it close, telling herself she was protecting her friend and not the other way around.

Laurie pointed out various sites to them. "Mother, that's the tallest skyscraper at the moment but not for long. According to the newspapers, they will build another one soon with a hundred floors. Maybe even two hundred."

Lily didn't look up as it made her dizzy. Instead, she looked around her as they moved through the streets. New York was changing so quickly and not just because they had finally brought all the little villages under one name. People were making money in this new age of construction. Unfortunately, the gap between those making money and those who lived in constant fear of becoming homeless was only getting wider. She closed her eyes firmly to get rid of the morbid thoughts. She would deal with those issues on Monday when she went to work at the sanctuary. This weekend was all about her family.

"Go faster, Charlie."

"Yes, ma'am," he replied, touching his cap and making the boys laugh. They drove to a soda fountain shop where they all indulged in cream sodas. Then it was off to have a drive along the river. In the distance they saw the various steamboats making their way up and down the river.

"That reminds me darling," Charlie said. "We have an invitation to cruise up the East River. One of our new partners, a German Jewish lawyer by the name of Cohen, invited us. You could make some useful contacts for the sanctuary. You should join us Kathleen, Richard and Patrick too if they are free."

"What's the occasion?" Lily asked. They didn't normally get invited to lawyer functions. Not the whole family. Charlie glanced at her.

"St. Mark's Lutheran church has an annual celebration. This year they have hired a steamboat called the General Slocum."

"After the hero of Gettysburg and Georgia?" a little voice piped up.

"Yes, Laurie, well done. See studying pays off, Teddy."

Teddy didn't reply. Lily hastened to change the subject. She didn't want Charlie and Teddy falling out today. Not on Teddy's birthday. Nora, Charlie's sister, had told her Charlie had no interest in books when he was younger, yet he was adamant his children would get a decent education to secure their future. Poor Teddy couldn't be less interested in books if he tried, while Laurie would read through the whole day and into the night if he was allowed.

"The reverend would like to invite some of the

orphans going on the next orphan train. He said it would give them something to remember New York. I agree, but I said I would have to give you the final say."

Lily acknowledged her husband's remark with a smile. She knew Charlie was a good man when she married him, but she had never imagined how much he would support her with the sanctuary. He never interfered and only offered his opinion when asked. He regularly told her how proud he was of what she and the others had achieved. And he didn't just tell her. The partners in the law firm had become donors to the sanctuary because of Charlie praising her efforts.

CHAPTER 7

They drove along the river and then back to their home. Once there, the rest of their friends had arrived for the twin's birthday party. Lily greeted Mini Mike and Tommy with affection but couldn't bring herself to do anything but smile at Granny Belbin. If she had a moment, she would tell the old lady what she could do with her tea leaves.

Inspector Griffin arrived without his wife. Lily wasn't surprised, she had only once met the woman and got the impression she didn't enjoy being in public. The inspector didn't seem to mind though, he was surrounded by friends and almost part of the family. Richard was waiting for them with Patrick.

"Wow, that's some car, can I drive it?" Patrick asked.

"Maybe wait until you are older, son," Richard told him. "Let Charlie get used to his new motor. Once it is less shiny and new looking, he might be more open to lending it out."

Patrick looked glum but when Charlie promised to take him for a drive around the block, his mood brightened. Before Lily could stop them, the men disappeared, leaving her with two fed up looking ten-year-olds. Teddy's lip jutted out, his eyes sparkling.

"It's our party. Why does Papa have to be the center of attention?"

"Teddy, I don't think it's your papa as much as his new toy. Come on inside and see your presents. I think you've waited long enough." Lily led the boys into the house, the rest of the guests following in their wake.

Teddy was overjoyed with his baseball bat, ball and cap. He was so excited that at first, he missed the tickets Richard and Kathleen had hidden inside the glove.

"Richard will take you, Laurie and Patrick to the game next weekend if you like."

"Thanks Aunty Kathleen. Look Laurie."

But Laurie was caught up in his own presents. Richard had bought him several books on different scientific subjects. But it was the newspaper Richard had included that grabbed his full attention. He was sprawled across the floor, one of the papers open on the floor as he read through it.

"Richard, you're the best. I can't wait to fly. Do you think if I wrote to the Wright brothers, they would let me up on the plane?"

Richard didn't have a chance to respond as Lily took over.

"I hope not Laurie. Some things are too dangerous for children."

Granny Belbin spoke up. "Never mind children, if God wanted us to fly, he would have given us wings."

For once Lily agreed with the old woman, not that she was about to admit it. She saw the look of disappointment on her son's face. She didn't have it in her to destroy his hopes and dreams. "Maybe when you are a little older, Laurie, and they have done more tests. You have plenty of time yet. Who knows what the next year will bring, never mind ten years?"

Granny Belbin gave her a significant look, but Lily ignored the old woman. She could keep her prophesies for disaster to herself. Thankfully, just at that moment, her husband and his friends arrived back to announce they were starving.

"Cook has outdone herself once more. Come and get it while it is hot. There is plenty." Lily moved around her friends to make sure everyone had a plate. When she got to inspector Griffin, she told him Cook had a basket prepared for his wife.

"That's so good of you Miss Lily. I wish she would come to your house, but she won't leave our home now. She is convinced the boys might find their way back home when we are out of the house. She can't accept they are long gone."

Lily rubbed his shoulder sympathetically. After the

meal, Granny Belbin wanted to go home. Lily didn't try to persuade her to stay. She was sick of the woman giving her funny looks all evening but Lily wasn't prepared to ask Granny if she had seen something horrible in the future. Lily didn't believe in that rubbish. Mike and Tommy left with Granny, they would make sure the old lady got home safe and sound. Lily gave Tommy five dollars to buy some coal and food for Granny. The woman may not be in her good books but she was a part of Lily's community and they looked after their own.

CHAPTER 8

*R*ichard stood up after the meal and tapped his spoon on his glass to gather everyone's attention.

"Thank you for hosting this gathering, Lily. Happy birthday to both Teddy and Laurie. Becoming ten years old is quite a big occasion, at least Kathleen and I think so. It should be marked accordingly. So, we would like to take the boys to Coney Island. There is a new adventure park open, it is big and scary enough to intrigue both boys. So, what do you think?"

Teddy jumped off his seat. "Please Mom, can we go? I want to see the fire exhibits. Laurie wants to see how the planets work. Can we, please?"

Lily glanced at Father Nelson. She wasn't sure how to react. Coney Island had a deservedly bad reputation during the last years of the 19th century, but most people believed that the governor had made great strides in cleaning it up. Still, she didn't want to cause any offense. Particularly when she and Father Nelson worked so closely on the sanctuary and orphan trains.

"I feel rather left out," Father Nelson surprised her by saying. "I would love to see the park too. Is there room for an old man?"

Lily stared at the priest who winked back at her.

"Father, we would love to have you. In fact, why don't we make it a sanctuary outing for next Friday? Perhaps we can close the sanctuary for the day." Richard glanced at Lily. "Well, maybe not close it fully, but leave someone in charge in case the sanctuary's services are needed. But the rest of us can all go. My treat."

Charlie protested. "Richard you can't bring everyone."

"I absolutely can. I have so much to be grateful for, most of all my wife Kathleen and son Patrick, neither of whom I would have met but for the sanctuary. Your friendship, all of you who supported us through everything. This is the least I can do. So, when shall we go? Lily, are the girls allowed to come with us?"

Lily glanced at her daughters. Neither seemed interested, Evie looked scared.

"Coleen is too young. Grace can go if she wants but Evie may prefer to stay home and help me watch Colleen." The look of relief on Evie's face told her she'd done the right thing.

"Oh no, Mom you have to go," Teddy insisted. "Leave Evie and Coleen with Cook."

"Theodore Doherty, that is not nice. Cook may want to come too."

"Oh no Miss Lily, you go right ahead. I've no time for that Coney Island business. I know what they says about that place and it's not fit for…" Cook trailed off as if realizing her next words could offend those present.

"Cook, if you are sure you don't mind. I'd love to go. Charlie and I had some dealings on the waterfront there years ago. It would be nice to see what has changed."

"You can tell us, Lily. I better not go, the Bishop might hear of my trip. Inspector, are you going?"

"No Father Nelson, I won't be going."

The children jumped up and down in excitement. Sarah, a girl from the sanctuary who helped her when the twins and Grace were babies, stood up. "Come on children, it's bedtime. Who will be first changed and washed up? You get to pick the story."

The boys muttered about it being babyish, but it didn't stop them racing out the door. Soon it was just the adults remaining. Lily suggested they adjourn to the sitting room where it was more comfortable. Cook stayed behind to clear up.

"Cook, come sit with us," Lily implored her. "We can clear away in the morning."

"Oh, no Miss Lily. You go ahead. I prefer to get my

kitchen tip top before I go to bed. Off you go now, you are getting under my feet."

Lily didn't argue. Despite it being her house, the kitchen had and always would belong to Cook.

CHAPTER 9

*A*s the adults made themselves comfortable, Lily coughed to attract their attention.

"While you are all here, I think it's a good idea to discuss our plans for the next orphan train. We have one hundred and twenty orphans ready to move. The first train of twenty will leave next week for Riverside Springs."

Father Nelson spoke first, "But where are we going to send the rest of them? Since the law changed in Missouri and other states, we can't afford to send that many at once. We have to ensure they won't be a burden on the state. That requires levels of funding we have yet to master."

Lily felt Father Nelson's frustration. Why did every decision come down to a lack of funds? "River-side Springs can take five now. In time they will take more. Bridget and Carl have been working hard, spreading news around the local neighborhoods. The local people have helped a lot in building the orphanage."

Inspector Griffin sat forward. "The police fundraiser went well. We raised about twenty-five dollars. I thought we would send that to Bridget to help her with the orphanage?"

Lily wanted to hug the Inspector, but Father Nelson spoke first.

"Congratulations on your efforts, Inspector, but I'm afraid of attracting bad press coverage if we move children from New York into orphanages. People want these kids to go to real homes."

Lily couldn't bite her tongue. "Those same people who refuse to give money to our fundraisers and would never welcome a child under their roof. They have a lot to say when they don't suffer hardship."

"True, Lily, but it's always been that way. Some things will never change. We just have to find a way around them. Now, if we were to maintain that Bridget's orphanage was a placing out home, i.e. one that would only house the children for a limited time until suitable homes were found for them, that might work."

"Father Nelson, are you suggesting we lie to your parishioners?" Lily pretended to be shocked.

"It's not a lie, my dear Lily. Our aim in time is for every orphan to find a suitable home. But for some, it may take a considerable amount of time. That time is best spent in the open fresh air of Riverside Springs rather than in the filthy disease-ridden tenements of our city."

Lily and Kathleen exchanged a grin. It wouldn't be the first-time Father Nelson had used fancy words to get around his wealthier parishioners' issues. But neither she nor Kathleen cared what it took for the rich to open their wallets.

The priest looked grave.

"What's wrong, Father Nelson?" Lily asked. "You have that look on your face."

"What look? Oh, never mind. I might as well tell you. We are very short staffed. I may have to delay sending the next group of orphans." Lily stared at him. The priest held up his hands. "I know we agreed next week but then Lucas Reynolds ended up in the hospital and will take a few weeks to recover. May Darcy is in Chicago and the men Lucas was training up are busy checking up on orphans placed over the last twelve months. We need more people, but few want to volunteer to escort groups of children for miles across the country."

Kathleen spoke up. "I will go with the next group of orphans. I miss Bridget and the others so much. Richard is busy at work, Patrick doesn't need me around all the time and Lily can handle the sanctuary with the help of other staff. It makes sense for me to go."

Richard turned to Kathleen. "Are you sure, darling? It's a very emotional experience."

"I'll be fine. I need to see my sister."

Father Nelson folded his arms. "Thank you, Kathleen. I am sure Jane will go with you, if we can tear her away from Gregory."

"Ah young love. Isn't Gregory the first man Jane has walked out with?" Lily asked.

"Yes, I believe so. Still he is a nice boy from a good family. I know his mother." Father Nelson sipped his tea.

"Jane doesn't need to come with me. If it's a small group. I can manage on my own."

"Kathleen, I know you are capable, but it is better if there are two of you," Lily said. She wished she could go with Kathleen but that was impossible. "It's a lot to take on. If Jane doesn't wish to go, maybe Richard could go with you?"

"I would love to, but I am busy at the hospital. What about Patrick?" Richard suggested.

"Our son is studying for his exams. I will be fine. Jane won't let us down. And I am sure there will be a couple of older children who can help with the younger ones. We can make sure to travel when George is working as conductor. He will help us. He is such a kind man."

Father Nelson nodded, a broad smile on his face.

"Kathleen, thank you. Lily, can you organize one of cook's baskets for George. Not that he needs to be bribed into helping us, but I know he appreciates her fine cooking."

Everyone smiled at Father Nelson. George wasn't the only man who liked Cook's baking.

"Are you sure, you won't come with us to Coney Island? I bought a couple of extra tickets for the train." Charlie focused his gaze on Father Nelson. The priest smiled but shook his head.

"Sorry Charlie but I think some of my parishioners would report me to the Bishop. I can't risk getting on his wrong side, he isn't too keen on me at the moment."

Lily couldn't believe it. Why would the Bishop have an issue with Father Nelson? The man went out of his way to help as many as he could. Before she could ask, Kathleen beat her to it.

"What have you done to upset the Bishop, Father Nelson?"

"What I have not done, Kathleen, would be the better question. The recent press coverage of the Orphan Trains has caused the Bishop some issues. He says he is fending off more charges of the Catholic Church condoning slavery."

"But that's ridiculous." Charlie stood up. "What sort of idiot believes that nonsense. Everyone in this room does their best for those children."

Lily caught her husband's eye and motioned for him to retake his seat.

"My apologies, Father Nelson. I didn't mean to insinuate your Bishop is an idiot."

"Charlie, I didn't argue with you, did I?" Father Nelson's eyes twinkled for a second before he became serious once more. "The Bishop has suggested I refrain from mixing our children with those of other faiths. He doesn't want Catholic children corrupted by others."

Lily had heard enough. "I swear to God that man is an idiot. Who cares what religion someone practices so long as they are good to the children? Surely it is more important to provide a safe and loving home rather than worry about what Church they attend?"

"I agree, Lily. I haven't told him we have two Jewish girls going on the next train. I also may have suggested to Reverend Haas, he come to meet you, Kathleen and your wonderful husbands. Reverend Haas is very interested in the work you do at the sanctuary."

"Funny you should mention him, Father. Charlie told us this evening he is organizing a big picnic and thought to invite us. Isn't that right, Charlie?"

Charlie nodded. "Yes Lily, they were talking about him at work."

"Reverend Haas decided young Pieter Fleming should ride our train," Father Nelson added.

"Is that the young boy who lost his parents in the trolley accident?"

"Yes Kathleen. Reverend Haas believes there are many more children who could benefit from being sent away from New York. Little Germany is experiencing a decline. Much like other places in New York. Those who enjoy a little bit of good fortune are taking their children to live in better neighborhoods. Where they can enjoy good housing, fine schools and less crime."

"Meanwhile the people left behind become poorer and more vulnerable," Kathleen said. "The Bishop should encourage his rich parishioners to do more to help to reduce crime. To get the gangs off the streets and into better paying jobs. To provide better housing. I bet some of his parishioners own the tenements those poor people call a home."

"Kathleen, maybe I should introduce you to the bishop."

Lily looked at the priest seeing the fresh lines around his eyes. He looked older every day. She had no idea what age he was.

"Why don't we invite Reverend Haas and his wife to dinner next week. Then we can discuss ways to work together. Father Nelson you can just happen to pop in. I don't have to tell your Bishop who comes to dinner in my home."

"Yes Lily, let's do that. Father Nelson, between Kathleen and my wife, I am sure they will find a way to work around your Bishop. For now, why don't we all have another drink and then I will drive Father Nelson home."

Father Nelson stood so quickly, he nearly knocked his chair over. "Thank you, Charlie, but I will get a cab. Your horseless carriage reminds me of my younger days hanging onto the back of a horse for dear life. I will leave you younger people to enjoy the rest of your evening. Just one last request."

"Yes Father," Lily replied.

"Bring me some Coney Island Taffy. I've heard great things about it."

Everyone burst out laughing at the childish joy on the Priests face.

"I will, Father. Maybe I will buy some for the Bishop too."

"Make his extra sticky. He can't lecture me if his mouth is full." Father Nelson tipped his hat, closing the door as he left the room.

"I wish I could speak to the Bishop." Lily's voice shook with anger. "Actually, I should kidnap him and make him live in a tenement. One night in a place like the hovel we found Toby and the other children in, and he might just change his mind."

"Lily, darling. Some will never change their ways. Don't lose sleep over that man. His time of reckoning will come."

"Do you really believe that, Charlie?" Kathleen asked as Richard sat beside her on the sofa.

"Yes, Kathleen. I might not go to church as regular as Father Nelson would like but I believe in God. We will all have to face his judgement one day. I would love to be present when the Bishop tries to explain to his master how he could have done more to help the children but didn't."

Lily knew Charlie believed every word he said but

she found it difficult to believe in a God who would let so many children and families suffer. With men like the Bishop in charge and with stories of how some nuns treated the orphan children, her belief in a higher power was tested on a daily basis. She didn't want to think about that now.

"So, Charlie, tell us about what we are going to see in Coney Island?"

She wasn't really interested but Charlie could talk forever about the new attractions. Richard and Kathleen seemed to enjoy the conversation. She hoped their visit would live up to Charlie's promises.

eddy, Laurie and their friends jumped up and down, sitting one minute and standing the next. They were so excited. Charlie had agreed to each of the twins bringing two friends to the show. Laurie had chosen Pieter, the latest arrival at the sanctuary and Teddy had brought his friend, Kevin. All four boys had already spent their allowance on candy. Instead of taking Charlies new automobile, they had taken the express train from Lower Manhattan. Pieter had never been on a train before. Nor had Kevin and the twins pretended they hadn't as they wanted to share in their friend's excitement.

It was a beautiful sunny day and the crowds were out in force. Lily made sure the boys knew where to go if they got separated from the adults. Charlie told her to relax but she was conscious of the number of strangers around them. That and the dubious reputation Coney Island had enjoyed in years gone by.

"Mom it's time to go in. We got to get our seats now or we will miss the opening."

"Relax Teddy, we have to wait our turn. You can't skip the queue." Lily turned to Teddy's friend. "Are you feeling all right, Kevin, you look a bit pale."

"I'm okay thank you, Mrs. Doherty." The boy clearly wasn't but at least he was making an effort. Lily sat beside him. She could take him outside if he got too scared. Pieter made a few remarks in German. Lily couldn't understand the words, but his expression of delight was easy to read. She was glad to see him smiling. She hoped Kathleen would find him a nice home when they traveled together on the orphan train.

"What is going to happen, Mom?" Laurie asked, not taking his eyes from the stage.

"I have no idea. Ask your father."

"Dad?" Laurie stood to get Charlie's attention.

Charlie read from the flyer in his hand. "The Fire and Flames exhibit will be like nothing you have ever seen before. Take a seat quickly, I think it's about to start."

The curtain raised. Lily was astonished to find herself looking at a full-sized New York style tenement. It looked just like it had been lifted out of Hells' Kitchen. In fact, she wouldn't have been surprised if Granny Belbin had appeared out of one of the windows. She looked at the people around her. Their obvious disappointment mirrored her own feelings. They hadn't come all the way to Coney Island to look at a depressing part of New York they could see every day for free if they wanted to.

Lily sat back and watched as life on the "street" in front of them unfolded. Street peddlers sold their wares with children playing in and out between their carts just like in real life.

"Mom, this is boring. Can we see something else?"

"Shush Teddy. Maybe something will—" Before Lily could finish her sentence, members of the audience screamed as smoke followed by flames poured out of the upper window of the tenement. Lily grabbed for her children's hands, wondering how they would reach the exit with all the people around them. Women and children near the tenement windows screamed. "We're trapped, help us."

Lily couldn't drag her eyes away from the scene in front of her. She heard the fire engine bells and soon there were dozens of firemen at the scene. They poured water onto the fire, while others wielding axes ran into the building.

"Mom, look," Teddy was jumping up and down as he pointed to some fireman laying out a tarpaulin. They gestured to the women and children to jump. Lily held a hand to her mouth as the victims did just that. Thankfully, the makeshift net held, and nobody fell to their death. Then it was all over. The curtain dropped, and the lights came on. The audience stood and clapped. Lily remained seated, not quite believing that what she had seen hadn't been real. It was all a pretense. Nobody had been in real danger.

"You look pale, darling. Are you not feeling well?" Charlie asked.

"I can't believe they would make up something so horrible about a fire. Real fires destroy lives every day. It isn't something they should use to entertain us." Lily could see her husband didn't agree with her sentiments. Frustrated, she looked around her. Kevin and Pieter were both clapping as enthusiastically as her children.

SHE SEEMED to be in the minority. Most of the audience seemed delighted by the performance, their faces lit up with joy. Maybe Lily had seen too much of the real life experienced by those in the tenements.

"Can we go home, please?" she asked.

"Aw Mom, not yet. I want to see the—"

"Teddy, stop it. Your mother is upset. Come on Lily, get your coat." Charlie took command of the situation and led their family out.

Her children left Lily in no doubt they blamed her for ruining their fun. But she couldn't change her mind. She thought the exhibit was tasteless. Just last

Christmas, over six hundred people had lost their lives in a fire at a theater in Chicago. What was the sense of making fun or entertainment from something so deadly?

CHAPTER 11

*W*hen they got to the exit, they found Richard and Kathleen waiting for them. Patrick soon arrived carrying some candy for the children.

"What did you think?" Kathleen whispered to Lily.

"It was horrible. Why would anyone want to see something like that?"

Kathleen linked arms with Lily. "I am so glad you feel like I did. I'm sure the people around me thought I was odd. They seemed to love it but all I could think about were the children we've sent out of New York on the trains because of fires."

"I think both you ladies need a holiday and time to recover your sense of fun. The organizers know New Yorkers love nothing better than tales of down-to-earth men becoming heroes. Firemen are those heroes. In fact, most of the men you saw on stage are real life fire-fighters making an extra few bucks acting out here." Charlie grinned at the two women. "I am guessing you wouldn't be up for going to see the Johnston flood reen-actment then?"

"Yay Dad, that sounds cool. Can we go there next? Laurie would love it and it would be good for lessons. We could tell the teacher all about it when we get back to school. Can we go? Now?" Teddy begged. "Kevin and Pieter want to go too. Don't you?" Teddy nudged the boys beside him, and they all looked imploringly at Charlie.

"Charlie Doherty. When will you learn to keep things to yourself?" Lily protested above the shouts of her twin boys.

"Boys will be boys," Kathleen said. "Maybe after you take the children to see the various enactments, you could bring them over to the firemen who will teach them about real fires and how dangerous they are."

Lily nodded in approval to Kathleen's suggestion. At least some good might come out of their visit. But, there was no way on this planet she was going to any more real-life reenactments. Where was a good old-fashioned magician or a singer?

"Richard, would you mind escorting Lily home and I will stay with the boys. Patrick, you can stay too if you like?"

"Thanks Mr. Doherty. I'd like that. Sorry Mom but I enjoyed it." Patrick kissed Kathleen on the cheek.

"Richard, do you want to stay too? Kathleen and I are well capable of taking the train back home?"

"No, thank you, Lily. I feel the same as you both do. Enjoy Charlie, boys. See you later, son."

Lily kissed her husband and boys goodbye and headed to the exit with Richard and Kathleen.

"Thank you Richard, I hope I didn't ruin your day out."

"Lily, you didn't. I was glad to leave. After dealing with burn victims day in and day out, I thought the exhibit rather tasteless to be honest. Kathleen wasn't too impressed either."

Kathleen didn't say anything. Lily glanced at her wondering what was on her friend's mind. She'd been all jittery since the visit to Granny Belbin. Was she worried about the Orphan Train?

"Kathleen, you with us?"

"Sorry Lily, I was miles away. Pieter is a lovely young boy isn't he. I wonder if I will be able to find a foreign, I mean German speaking family for him."

Lily wasn't convinced it was Pieter's situation bothering her friend, but she wasn't about to say so. "You might find a family like Kevin's. Couldn't get one more American yet they speak German as a family. Kevin's grandparents on both sides came over in the 1860's."

They chatted about this and that as they made their

way home. Kathleen and Richard didn't linger. Lily enjoyed having the house to herself as Sarah had taken the other children out. Lily took out a book intending to read but was fast asleep when the boys finally came home.

WHEN THEY GOT HOME, Laurie and Teddy escaped up to their rooms. When Lily checked on them later, she found them playing firemen. Teddy was the fireman and Laurie the child who needed rescuing.

As the paper coverage proved over the next few days, Lily and Kathleen were in the minority. Most people loved the Fire and Flames experience. Most everyone she came in contact with had either seen it for themselves or heard of it from their neighbors.

Charlie took the paper from her hands one evening, not long after they had seen the event. Wrapping his arms around her, he kissed the side of her neck.

"Darling, you've forgotten the most important thing about the show. It gives New Yorkers what they want most from life. A happy resolution to every problem."

Distracted by her husband's caresses, Lily didn't argue. Who was she to stop others from having their fun?

CHAPTER 12

Kathleen and Lily were sitting in the sanctuary office, checking the final preparations for the next orphan train.

"Thank you so much for not pulling out of accompanying this train," Lily said. "I think no one could have borne it if we'd had to cancel the trip again."

Kathleen agreed. "The children are nervous enough without the train being canceled at the last minute. I said from the start I could handle it alone, but I had hoped, if I'm honest, Jane would come with me. It's a pity Gregory convinced her to elope. They could have gotten married first and taken the orphans to Green River as part of their honeymoon trip."

Lily smiled at Kathleen's attempt at a joke. "I hope she will be happy. Gregory seems to be a nice man, but

I wouldn't like to live with my mother-in-law. Especially, if I hadn't met her."

"I thought you got on well with Charlie's mother."

"Ruth is a lovely woman, but I like the fact she lives in Clover Springs and not in New York. Mothers always think the sun shines out of their children. I love Charlie, but some days he just drives me nuts."

"Isn't that what all men do?" Kathleen asked.

"Ladies, do I feel my ears burning?"

Father Nelson stepped into the room. "Sorry to intrude but Cook let me in. She said to make my way through, she's in a tizzy. She's run out of sugar or something for her baking."

"Poor Cook," Lily said. "She is making a batch of cookies for the children to celebrate their last night. She made the mistake of asking them which ones they would like, and they all chose different types."

"I hope someone asked for coconut and chocolate. They are my favorites." Father Nelson subconsciously rubbed his expanding belly.

"I think Cook knows better than to forget you, Father Nelson. It's lovely to see you but why are you here? Something tells me you are about to change our plans."

"Lily Doherty, are you implying I would interfere with any of your arrangements?"

Lily just lifted her eyebrows, making Father Nelson blush a little.

"Well, Lily, maybe I do. This one can't be

helped. Kathleen, I need you to collect another child on the trip. She will join you at a small station two stops farther down the line. There was no time to collect her and bring her to the sanctuary."

"What's her name, her age?" Kathleen asked.

"Mia Chambers, and she is six years old. I made a big mistake."

Surprised, Kathleen and Lily both looked at the old priest.

"When her parents died in a tenement fire a year ago, Mia spent some time in the hospital. Three months ago, I persuaded her uncle to take custody of her. I shouldn't have. He is a young single man and obviously not equipped to deal with a six-year-old girl. He wrote and asked me to collect her. The poor child has lost someone else."

Lily looked confused. "I don't remember Mia. Did she come to the sanctuary?"

"No, the hospital released her into the care of the orphanage," the priest explained. "It was only when I met the uncle when he visited one day, that I asked him to take Mia. I felt sorry for her. I let my emotions cloud my vision."

"Father Nelson, you did the right thing," Lily said. "We always try to keep children with their families. At least you tried."

The priest looked up, and the sadness in his eyes tore at Kathleen's heart. She moved toward him and put her hand on his arm. She would have hugged him but for the collar he wore. That small white band put a distance between them. She rubbed his arm. "Father Nelson, Lily is right. You did what you thought best. I will collect Mia and find her the best family I can. I promise."

Father Nelson put his hand over Kathleen's. "Thank you my dear. I know you will do your best. There is nobody I trust more than you two ladies. Well apart from Bridget."

Kathleen saw the tears shining in his eyes and decided to try and lighten the mood.

"Well, that's lovely. My precious sister always has to take center stage even when she is hundreds of miles away." Kathleen puffed out her chest trying to appear indignant, but Lily's giggles were contagious. Both of them dissolved into laughter leaving Father Nelson looking a little bewildered. But at least he wasn't teary eyed anymore.

CHAPTER 13

$\mathcal{F}$rieda Klunsberg looked up from the kitchen sink. The dishes were almost done, and her father had yet to come home. He was always late these days. He spent money they didn't have on a beer or two before he came home. He said it was his way of coping with his losses. Frieda swirled the wash brush viciously. It wasn't just his losses. What about theirs?

Life had been much better with *Mutti* around. In the year since her mother's funeral, things had gone from bad to worse. Her father was talking about going back to Germany but that was a pipe dream. Passages cost money.

Hans, her ten-year-old brother, was faring the worst. He worked hard as a newsie. He used his money to buy papers and then stood on the corner until they were all sold. His meager earnings helped Frieda put food on the table. But not much of it.

"Frieda, I'm hungry," her brother complained. "Can't you give us something to eat?"

"You've just eaten. We don't have anything else. Have a drink of water."

"That's not going to fill me up. Can't I have some of that?" Hans eyed the remains of the pie sitting waiting for their father.

"No, you can't. Father will be hungry, and he's been working all day."

"I've been working too," he insisted. "I sold all my newspapers. I didn't let the bigger boys take my money either. I should eat more."

Frieda glanced toward their younger sister, Charlotte, although everyone called her Lottie. She never complained, although she was bound to be hungry too. As she watched, Lottie pushed her plate toward Hans. "Eat the rest, I'm not hungry."

Even as Hans made to grab the pitiful remains, Frieda smacked him over the head. "Don't steal her food. Look at her, she gets thinner by the day."

"Ouch, you didn't have to hit me so hard. It's not my fault she's sick. She should be in the hospital. You heard the reverend, but Papa won't let her go."

Frieda turned back to the sink. She knew why their father didn't want his daughter in the hospital. That was where *Mutti* and Otto had died, and he blamed the nurses and doctors at the hospital. Frieda pushed the hair back from her head. She should be out working but her father refused to let her. Said she had to stay and mind Lottie. But if she had a job, she would be able to buy better food and Lottie would get healthier.

The door banged shut behind Hans. She thought about going after him, but it was pointless. He would be long gone. Probably down to the river front with his mates. He was growing wild. The soft, kind-hearted boy had disappeared when Mutti had died to be replaced by the stone faced ten-year-old who acted like the weight of the world was on his shoulders.

"Come on Lottie," she said, attempting to shake herself out of her thoughts, "let's go out on the roof. It will be cooler."

Although Frieda loved the sun, she hated summer in the tenements. The heat of the day seemed to seep into the building only to be released in the evenings. It never grew cool. She thought longingly of their child-hood village in Bavaria, of the cool summer evenings and the lovely lake to swim in during the day. The only way they could swim in New York was to take a risk on the East River, but thoughts of the filthy water, never mind the risk from being hit by one of the many boats sailing up and down, was enough to deter her. The only other option was to attend one of the many pools being built, but they cost money. It seemed an awful lot of effort for fifteen minutes of swimming time.

"I'm too hot Frieda. It stinks too."

Frieda picked up the five-year-old girl, her lack of weight another sign she was wasting away. "I know *Liebling*, but it will be better outside on the roof. Just you wait and see."

CHAPTER 14

*F*rieda carried her sister to the roof. There they met lots of other children with the same idea, some with their families.

"Evening Frieda, how is Lottie doing today?"

"Same, Mrs. Sauer. She isn't eating very much but I hope the air up here will help her. It gets very warm in our rooms."

"You should be out having some fun not stuck at home minding Lottie, Frieda. You know I will watch her for you if you want to go out."

Frieda knew Mrs. Sauer would do anything for their family. Her mother and Mrs. Sauer had grown up together and been firm friends until *Mutti* had died.

"I would like to get a job, but *Papi* won't listen to me. He says I must stay home like a respectable German girl."

"*Ja*, your father has some old-fashioned opinions."

"He still thinks we live in Bavaria," Frieda said. "Here in New York, people work. All my friends from school have jobs. I am fourteen now. I'm not a child."

"Oh, my poor *Liebling*," Mrs. Sauer said, "but you will always be a child in your father's eyes. At least until you leave home and get married. But, here in America, they do things differently from back home in Germany. This is why we came here. But your father, he forgets what it was like to be young. Do you want me to speak to your father?"

Frieda shook her head. Her father wouldn't like Mrs. Sauer interfering. But the woman wouldn't be put off.

"I will speak to Reverend Haas. He is a good, sensible man and your father will listen to him. Now, why don't you leave Lottie with me for a while and you find your friends? Have a chat. Go on now. I have some fruit my Heinrich brought home from the market. He couldn't sell it, it is too bruised and looks too ugly for his customers. But inside it tastes the same. It will do your sister good. Go on now."

Frieda checked to make sure Lottie was comfortable. Her sister loved Mrs. Sauer. She thanked the lady again before moving across the roof to find the girls she'd known from school. She spotted Marthe Dunst but wasn't quick enough to turn back to Mrs. Sauer as the girl had seen her.

"Frieda, there you are. Have you heard the news?"

Frieda took a seat and waited for Marthe to tell her. It was never a good idea to steal Marthe's thunder. With her long blonde hair and clear blue eyes, she was a favorite among the boys. And the adults, who all believed her to be an angel. She wasn't, far from it, but she was good at not getting caught. Frieda hadn't liked Marthe at school but *Mutti* had insisted she play with the girl, telling Frieda she only acted the way she did because she was lonely. Her parents were older, and she didn't have any siblings to play with.

"Reverend Haas is organizing a great big party in one month's time. It is on Wednesday, June 15th. Everyone is invited." Marthe stole a glance at Frieda. "Well, those with money to buy the tickets."

Frieda ignored the gibe. She would not let Marthe get under her skin. She had bigger worries. Her reaction seemed to spur Marthe on even more. Frieda dug her nails into the palms of her hands at the gloating look in Marthe's eyes.

"He will take us down the river on a ship. Everyone from church is going. We will dress in our finest clothes and pack a picnic. *Mutti* said she will buy me a new dress."

Frieda held Marthe's gaze but said nothing. Silence could speak volumes, at least that was what *Mutti* used to say. Frieda watched as a red patch spread up from Marthe's neck. She didn't think it was from the heat of the evening.

One of the girls spoke up, catching Marthe's attention, "I thought you were moving to Yorkville."

Marthe glared at Frieda before turning the biggest smile on the girl who had spoken up.

"We are. To a big house with its own front door. It's wonderful. I will have my own room. My mother's sister will live next door. Yorkville is so nice to live in. It's not smelly like here and we won't have to go on the roof to find some air."

The girls around Marthe sighed, almost collectively. Everyone from the area knew someone who had moved to Yorkville or elsewhere for a better standard of living. Only those who had to live in the tenements did so. But they dreamed of escaping. Frieda couldn't stand the gloating anymore.

"Yet you will come back here for the picnic." As soon as she spoke, she regretted it. She saw the gleam of triumph in Marthe's eyes. The other girl had gotten under Frieda's skin and they both knew it.

"Everyone who moved to Yorkville will come back. We have to do our best to support the reverend. *Mutti* has bought four additional tickets to give to those who can't afford to go. She says I can bring a friend."

Frieda looked away from the gleam in Marthe's eyes. She wasn't about to beg for charity, no matter how fabulous the picnic sounded.

The other girls surged closer to Marthe.

"Pick me, please."

"No, pick me. You know we've been friends

76

forever. I used to do your hair at school, remember? You liked to wear it in braids."

Frieda listened to her neighbors begging for the spare ticket but remained silent. It took all self control not to say something. It was so unfair, some families could afford to buy spare tickets when others couldn't bring together enough pennies to buy one. She felt Marthe's stare. She wasn't about to look at her but that was a sign of weakness. Gritting her teeth, she looked at her tormentor. Marthe's eyes gleamed.

"What about you Frieda? Wouldn't you like to go?'

"No, thank you Marthe, but it is kind of you to offer. I must get back to Lottie. If I don't see you before you move, I hope Yorkville works out well for you."

Frieda allowed herself a small sense of satisfaction as her words took the other girl by surprise. What had *Mutti* said? You could always kill badness with kindness. She strolled back to Mrs. Sauer.

"Back already? You didn't stay long."

"No, but thank you for looking after Lottie for me, Mrs. Sauer." Frieda tried to inject a note of enthusiasm into her voice when, in reality, she just wanted to go back into their room and hide. Maybe she could fall asleep and dream of a new life for all of them.

CHAPTER 15

*M*rs. Sauer put an arm around Frieda's shoulders and whispered so the other neighbors wouldn't hear. It didn't do to make enemies in a small community and Marthe's mother held grudges.

"You shouldn't let Marthe get under your skin, *Liebling*. She is an unhappy soul and her mission in life seems to be to spread this unhappiness."

Frieda tried to pretend Marthe hadn't upset her.

"She was trying to be kind. Her mother has bought extra tickets for Reverend Haas's trip. She offered me one."

"But the price was too high?"

"No, it was free." But even as she said the words, she realized Mrs. Sauer knew that with Marthe there was no such thing as free. Everything came with a price.

"I am glad you said no. Some prices are too high." Mrs. Sauer took a bite of her apple. As she chewed and spoke, bits of apple flew out of her mouth. "Do you want to go to this picnic?"

Frieda stared at the women. Was that a trick question? The whole of Little Germany wanted to go on the trip.

"Yes, but *Papi* will be working."

"And you don't have money to buy the tickets. Don't look embarrassed Frieda, we are in the same position. I am lucky. My husband and my two sons work, but we don't have the money to pay for such outings. Even if we did, we couldn't afford the loss of the income from closing the stall for a full day. But our time will come and so will yours. Now sit awhile and tell me about your studies. I heard you want to be a nurse. Have some apple–it's sweet and you can wipe the dirt off on your dress. See?" Mrs. Sauer wiped the apple across her ample bosom and took another bite. She handed a red apple with brown bruises to Frieda. Her stomach growled, her cheeks growing warmer knowing Mrs. Sauer had guessed she was hungry. She was tempted to keep the apple for Hans.

"Eat Frieda. You must keep your strength up. Your father relies on you even though he doesn't realize it. You are the strong one in your family. Your mother, God rest her soul, knew that from the day you were placed in her arms. Now what are you waiting for? Eat."

Frieda bit into the juicy apple. She didn't care if it was overripe or badly bruised, it was the most delicious thing she had eaten in days.

"So, what are you doing about your future?" Mrs. Sauer prompted.

Had *Mutti* told her friend of Frieda's dreams to be a doctor? Her *Mutti* had told her to aim for the sky and not let anyone try to put her off. She'd promised to work on *Papi,* but now she was dead and *Papi* wouldn't listen to anyone.

"*Papi* doesn't agree with women studying. He says it is better for a woman to know her place and raise a family."

"*Ja*, it is," Mrs. Sauer agreed.

Frieda's stomach turned over. She'd expected a little support from Mrs. Sauer. She didn't think the woman would be so old-fashioned.

"Frieda, it is a good life for the girls who want to be mothers and wives. You may want that in time too, but for now you wish to study. So, you must work on this. You can go to the library while your father is at work. I can mind Lottie until you come back."

A flare of hope burned bright for about two seconds. "Thank you, but I can't ask you to do that. Father wouldn't like it."

"What your father doesn't know can't hurt him." Mrs. Sauer looked around and then, lowering her voice, said, "Sometimes us women have to do things the men don't agree with. It is for their own good we don't tell them. They cannot worry about what they don't know, right?"

Frieda wasn't at all sure it was a good thing, but Mrs. Sauer continued, "I am not telling you to defy your father. I wouldn't condone that. I wouldn't allow you to sneak off with a boy. But getting an education, that's a good thing. You will learn in time that sometimes those who love us try to protect us too much from the world. Your father is scared. He has lost your mother, and he has lost belief in the new country he thought would be the answer to his prayers. When he left his family behind in Germany, it wasn't so he could bring up his family in this." Mrs. Sauer swept her arms around. "He wanted more for you. But he cannot see the way forward to freedom is by education."

"How come you see it?" Frieda asked.

"Me? My father was a school teacher, but my mother was a reader. She read many books and told us the stories. It was she who told me to go to America. She said I must teach my children to read. But my boys?" Mrs. Sauer shrugged her shoulders. "They would rather play ball or chase girls than read a book."

Frieda giggled at the expression on Mrs. Sauer's face and the older woman laughed too.

Frieda wondered if the plan would work. Could it be a chance for her to escape from her everyday life? She loved Lottie, but it was boring staying in their room day in day out. She'd read her mother's few books over and over. Reading gave her a chance to escape into another world.

"I tell you what, Frieda. Why don't we all go to the Astor library tomorrow? We can put Lottie in Jacob's carriage. He won't mind sharing, will you?" Mrs. Sauer bounced her latest baby on her knee. "See, he thinks it's a grand idea."

"You are kind, but they won't let the likes of me borrow books."

"Why? You think they only let rich people into the library? Mr. Astor, he was German you know. A good man, he set up the library for everyone. I know he is long gone but the books are still there. We go tomorrow. Early, when it is not too hot. Yes?"

"Yes." Butterflies filled her stomach at the thought of picking out new books to read. Oh, she hoped Mrs. Sauer was right. If they said she couldn't borrow the books, it would be horrible.

CHAPTER 16

Frieda sat enjoying the last of her apple, her mind working to remember which books her teacher had mentioned before. She'd loved school and Miss Lynch, an Irish teacher, had told her it was a pleasure to teach her. At first, after *Mutti* had died, Miss Lynch had called to their rooms and brought books and other presents.

But the neighbors teased Frieda's father that the unmarried teacher was looking for a husband and that had been the end of the visits. Frieda had snuck out a few months ago and gone to the school but Miss Lynch had left for pastures new. The replacement teacher wasn't interested in Frieda. All she did was complain how rude the class was and how she would bring them into line.

"Has your father given any more thought to the

orphan trains?" Mrs. Sauer's question made Frieda sit up. "You and Hans would get a new chance at a good life. Lottie, she couldn't go, but maybe if you and Hans got placed, your father would see sense and put her in the fever hospital. The doctors there can do great things for her."

Frieda tried to look surprised, but there was little point in pretending she hadn't heard her father discussing the orphan train with Mr. Sauer. *Papi* had assumed she was asleep. She had pretended she was so she could find out what his intentions were. She couldn't believe he thought sending her and Hans away was a good thing for their family. She knew things were tough, but if she got a job that would be a better answer than splitting the family up.

"Rev. Haas has some good friends in the other religious communities. One, a Catholic priest called Father Nelson, has sent several children on the orphan trains to a place called Riverside Springs. From descriptions it sounds like the village your *Mutti* and I grew up in. A small, but growing community who look out for each other. You could do well in such a place. You could become a teacher or work with the town doctor. Then, in time, you could meet a nice boy, maybe not a German one, but we are in America now. *Ja?*"

Frieda didn't want to think about meeting any husband, German or otherwise. She didn't want to offend her mother's friend either. She stayed silent.

"I know you want to stay together as a family, and I understand. But sometimes you have to do things for the good of everyone. Your father is working himself to death, Hans is running a little wild and you, my dear Frieda, look old before your time. Think about it. Even just a little. Many children leave New York on the orphan trains and find wonderful new lives. Did you hear young Pieter Fielding is going away soon."

Frieda nodded. Pieter was friends with Hans. She liked the solemn young boy who hadn't lived in America that long. She remembered his smiling face when Hans had brought him to their apartment to say hello. Pieter had smiled a lot back then. Back before his parents had been killed by the run away trolley.

Mrs. Sauer continued talking.

"You could find a family who supports you in your wish to study nursing. Your father will never allow it. We both know he is too old-fashioned for that."

Frieda didn't want to discuss the orphan train but didn't want to upset the woman who'd just given her the best idea ever. She stood up, brushing her hand down her dress to get rid of any residue from the apple. Surprised her mother's friend was encouraging her to go against her father's wishes, Frieda thought she better take Lottie back downstairs. Sometimes Lottie repeated things she had heard.

"Thank you, Mrs. Sauer. I will consider it. I best get Lottie back downstairs before *Papi* comes home. Have a nice evening."

Mrs. Sauer didn't persuade her to stay on the roof. Maybe she knew Frieda needed to process what she had been told. She would speak to *Papi* again tonight about Lottie. Her cough wasn't getting any better and anywhere had to be better than living here.

CHAPTER 17

The next morning, Frieda walked through the streets of Little Germany trying to stretch her budget. Papi had complained she didn't know much about shopping or cooking. Last night, he'd been in a foul mood and everything had been her fault. Usually she got up early to cook him some breakfast but this morning, she'd stayed in bed. Let him look after himself for one morning and then he might appreciate her efforts. But even as she thought the brave words, she felt guilty. Her father was working hard, the least she could do was be a good daughter.

"Frieda, smile. It's a beautiful day."

Frieda looked up at the woman smiling at her, from behind her vegetable stall. Come rain or shine, Mrs. Stellman was always found in this same spot. She primarily sold fruit and vegetables but would also sell some items on behalf of her neighbors. She had sold some of *Mutti's* handkerchiefs saying her customers loved *Mutti's* embroidery skills. Frieda wished she had paid attention when her mother had tried to teach her the same skills. Maybe then she would be able to earn some money from home.

"Morning Mrs. Stellman. Do you have anything for me today? I was hoping to make some soup. Lottie finds it easier to eat."

Frieda hated using her sister's illness but she didn't want to admit soup was cheaper to prepare.

"You have come to the right stall. These old vegetables, I think they must have been used as footballs. Look how mushy they are. But they would be good in a soup. How about a dime for this bag?"

Frieda opened her mouth to protest but quickly closed it. Mrs. Stellman was known for driving a hard bargain. The stall owner would make a profit on her other trades.

"Thank you Mrs. Stellman. They would be perfect."

"Good girl. Make sure you add plenty of salt. Can't bear a tasteless soup. You should see Mr. Wagner, I heard he has some marrow bones going cheap. They would nourish young Lottie."

Her cheeks flushing, Frieda tried to hide her embarrassment. Mrs. Stellman was trying to be kind but she wished everyone didn't know just how hard things were for Frieda's family.

"Frieda, we all have our troubles. God doesn't send

you anything he doesn't believe you can handle. Some say the more God loves you the more hardship he sends to you."

I wish he didn't love me quite so much. Frieda blinked quickly to get rid of her thoughts Thankfully she hadn't spoken aloud. Mrs. Stellman was still staring at her but her eyes were now full of concern. Frieda hastened to make the kind woman feel better.

"Thank you Mrs. Stellman. I had a silly fight with someone and it put me in a black mood. I feel better now. I will go and see the butcher right now."

CHAPTER 18

As Frieda moved toward the butchers, she couldn't help thinking there was nowhere better to live than Little Germany. Her neighbors were kind and really cared about her family.

Before she reached the butchers, Frieda bumped into Mary Abendschein, the main organizer of the Sunday school party. Frieda liked the kindly unmarried lady who was involved in every committee and activity in their parish. Mary had given Frieda clothes and food on occasion and sympathized with her over the death of her mother.

"Are you coming to the outing, Frieda?"

"No, Miss Abendschein. I have to stay home and look after Lottie."

"You could bring her too, it would be nice for her to get onto the river and breathe some fresh air. The picnic grounds at Locust Grove on Long Island are wonderful. Just the thing to brighten Lottie's spirits. George Maurer and his band, you know them, will play too."

Frieda knew she wasn't expected to answer. She didn't get a chance as Mary continued to speak. "We have plenty of food and drink for everyone and it will be safe too. I have two off duty New York policeman coming along to help make sure." Mary inclined her head to one side as if in deep thought. "Perhaps I should speak to your father."

Papi wouldn't like the woman coming to speak to him. Mary was in charge of fundraising and everyone knew she could push pennies out of most people. It was hard to resist her sweet nature.

"*Papi* works very hard at the moment. He rarely comes home. Says the demand for shoes to be fixed is bigger than normal," Frieda said.

"He is good at his job. There aren't many cobblers and shoemakers like your father. I will try to have a quick word though as I don't want you children missing out on a day of fun. I best get going, Frieda. Have a good day."

Frieda watched as the woman bustled off down the street. Miss Abendschein never walked anywhere. She was always moving quickly from here to there. Never stopping. Frieda wondered why she didn't have a family of her own. Maybe she made up for the loss of a husband and children by keeping busy for the church.

Frieda walked slowly back to their home, feeling very low. The everyday noises round her seemed louder, the incessant rumble of the trolley cars, the police whistles, shouts from vendors trying to sell their goods. The sheer competition from everyone just to survive. Added to the noise was the intense heat. Everyone seemed to move faster and faster. Bicycles and strollers fought for space on the pavements. The heat radiated from the ground and the surrounding buildings to the point that it was unbearable. The combination of heat and disgusting smells from the overflowing privies was enough to make her retch. How she longed to get away, if only for a few hours.

Maybe she should speak to *Papi*. She picked up her skirt and almost ran to the butchers. Mrs. Stellman had been right. Mr. Wagner gave her a huge bone and also threw in some additional meat, he said it was only fat but she could see it wasn't. She wanted to hug the large built man whose belly moved when he laughed but that wouldn't be appropriate.

"Thank you Mr. Wagner. I will ask Lottie to draw you a picture."

"Ja, please. She draws lovely pictures. See? I still have the last one." He pointed to a childish drawing of a family outside a house. Tears pricked her eyes as Frieda looked at her sister's drawing. Lottie missed *Mutti* most of all.

She choked out a goodbye and hurried home. She had some savings, pennies she had built up while

Mutti was ill. Her mother had always kept a small amount of coins in a jar under the floorboards. When she first got sick, she had shown it to Frieda. Nobody else knew about it, not even her father. As she hurried up the stairs to their rooms, she wondered how much the tickets were. She had forgotten to ask. Marthe's face flashed into her mind. She could bite down her pride and ask the girl for a ticket. Maybe even two. Then Hans and Lottie could go. She would find the money for her own ticket. She burst through the door of their room frightening Lottie.

"What's wrong? Is Hans in trouble again?" her sister asked.

"No darling, sorry. I was just in a hurry. How are you feeling? Did you sleep?"

Lottie nodded but closed her eyes again and fell back onto the covers. Today she was as pale as could be. Frieda waited a couple of minutes, impatiently moving from one foot to another. Only when she was certain the younger girl was asleep did she go to find her hidden box. She carefully emptied it onto the floor. There was almost a dollar. Would that be enough?

CHAPTER 19

*G*rand central Station

Lily hugged Kathleen. "Give Bridget a kiss from me. Ask her to write soon. Tell them all to write more."

"I will," Kathleen promised. "Now get off the train or you will end up coming with us."

As if someone heard her, the train guards blew a whistle. "Oh wait, let me off. Come on Teddy, Laurie. Say goodbye."

Laurie dashed off the train. "I want to see the engines move. I will be at the top of the platform as far as the guard will let me, Mom." He was gone before Lily could stop him.

His twin looked devastated. "Please, can I come with you, Aunty Kathleen? I promise to be good. I can sit with Pieter Fielding. He doesn't speak much English so I can help him."

Kathleen hid a smile. She knew Teddy didn't speak German so would have a difficult job of helping Pieter but still it was kind of him to think of the child. She drew him close.

"Teddy darling, you know only orphans come on the trains. You have a lovely family."

Teddy stamped his foot. "It's not fair. The orphans get all the fun. I want to go on an adventure. It's boring staying at home and having to go to school."

Kathleen glanced at Lily. She didn't want the orphans around them to hear her pointing out that the life Teddy enjoyed was just what the children she was taking away wanted. Her chance to be diplomatic was stolen by Cindy, a twelve-year-old girl.

"You're a stupid boy. You should be grateful you get to stay in your home. We have to go and live with strangers."

"I'm not stupid. You're stupid." Teddy glared at Cindy who laughed at him.

"Course you are. You have a ma like Miss Lily and all you do is moan. You haven't lived on the streets have ye? You ain't gone to bed hungry or had all you owned stolen in the night. Go home little boy." Cindy dismissed him with a scathing look before moving down the car to find her gang. Kathleen sighed. She knew Cindy's character had protected her on the streets, but she wished with all her heart that the girl wasn't so hard on those around her. She pulled Teddy closer, partly to save him from embarrassment. His eyes gleamed with unshed tears and she knew he would hate to be seen crying in public.

"Maybe next time I go to Riverside Springs, your parents will let you come on a holiday."

"Would you ask them? Please Aunty Kathleen, Mom listens to you."

"I'll ask," Kathleen said. "But first you have to behave. Now dry your eyes quickly and get off the train. Your mother is needed at home. Go on now. Chest out. Bridget, my sister, will probably have a gift for you seeing as she missed your birthday. Maybe a baseball?"

Teddy's eyes lit up, all thoughts of Cindy forgotten. "You're the best. Come on Mom, we have to get off." He was gone before Lily could respond.

"You have a gift with children, Kathleen Green. Mind you, young Cindy will try your patience," Lily warned.

"I know. She reminds me of Jacob. Do you remember how he was when we first met him? He didn't trust anyone either. It's not Cindy's fault. The things that child has seen."

"I know but she has to learn to put her best foot forward. Otherwise, placing her will be a nightmare," Lily said.

Kathleen looked back at Cindy. The young girl knew she was being observed; Kathleen had seen the child's hands turn to fists, yet she didn't look up. She hoped she had time to earn the girl's trust.

The whistle shrilled once more, and the train guard approached Lily.

"Come on Miss Lily, get off now or I will have to sell you a ticket."

Kathleen smiled as Lily greeted the conductor like an old friend. She knew so many people.

"Sorry George, got carried away chatting for a change. How's Mildred?"

"That cat will be the death of me, Miss Lily. The missus says she needs to be spoiled. Mildred is supposed to be a working cat, but I never seen her catch anything more than a nap on me favorite chair."

Lily and Kathleen giggled. One orphan had smuggled his cat, Mildred, onto the train last year. The kind-hearted conductor had promised to take good care of her when the orphan's new family couldn't take the animal.

"Now Miss Lily, last chance. Go on. I will look after Miss Kathleen and her little darlings."

"Thanks George, I know you will." Lily kissed the conductor on the cheek, hugged Kathleen and waved goodbye to the orphans. She got off just in time as the train surged forward.

CHAPTER 20

*K*athleen waved goodbye through the window before offering a quick prayer that her chat with Cindy would go well.

"Cindy, can you come and sit with me for a while, please?"

The girl looked up, her expression suggesting she would refuse.

"Please, Cindy." Kathleen used a firmer tone. She couldn't afford to be seen to lose control at this early stage of the journey. "I need your help with some younger children."

Cindy caved as Kathleen knew she would. Inside the hard-hearted front was a loving child who had a reputation for protecting younger kids on the streets.

"What?"

"Don't speak to me like that please, Cindy."

Cindy stared at Kathleen who returned her gaze.

She would not let the child have the upper hand and they both knew it. Kathleen struggled to maintain her stare, biting her inside lip to restrain the urge to laugh. Finally, the child backed down.

"Sorry," Cindy said. "Yes, Miss Kathleen?"

Kathleen ignored the defiant tone. Cindy had to win some arguments to keep her spirit. She would need that to survive.

"I know we spoke about how the orphan trains work, but I wanted to check if you had questions."

Cindy gazed at her hands.

"Cindy ?"

"What does it matter if I got questions. You ain't going to answer them. Nothing I can do to change things. If someone wants me, I got to go with them. If they don't, I got to go back to New York. Simple enough."

Kathleen pushed away the urge to hug the child and promise her it wouldn't be that bad. To tell her the train offered her a new life, one full of hope, love and shelter. But she couldn't. She refused to lie to the children. It wouldn't help and she wanted them to know they could trust her.

"Cindy, I can't make promises about how your new life will turn out. I will do my best to make sure you find a good home."

The girl wiped the snot from her nose on her sleeve. Kathleen pretended she hadn't noticed the scars on her arm. Cindy caught her gaze and held it. "Why?"

"I don't understand Cindy. Why what?"

"Why do you care? You get paid no matter what home I end up in."

"Paid?" Kathleen asked, eyebrows rising in surprise. "I don't earn any money for placing you and the other children in homes. Whatever gave you that idea?"

"I can read. A bit anyway. The papers say you sell us orphans and it pays for your big houses and your fancy clothes."

Kathleen could have swung for the reporters who printed silly stories to sell their newspapers. Didn't they have any real news to report?

"Cindy, the stories you have heard of us selling children are not true. I dress the way I do because I am lucky to have a doctor as a husband. Richard works in a hospital and earns a good salary. I work as a volunteer with the sanctuary."

"You mean you don't get paid to do this?" Cindy asked. "You're a dope."

Kathleen could tell the girl meant what she said. Why would anyone do anything for free?

"I didn't always work for nothing. About twelve years ago, I wasn't much older than you and I lived a similar life to yours."

"Yeah and watch your head as a pig might fly into

it. I know I ain't got a fancy schooling but I ain't stupid."

"I never said you were," Kathleen said. "I grew up in what they call Hell's Kitchen. I was lucky. I had an older sister, Bridget, who looked out for me. There were seven of us and she watched over all of us. We ended up in the sanctuary. Lily took us in, and I firmly believe she saved our lives."

Kathleen watched as Cindy's curiosity battled with her pretended indifference. Curiosity won.

"For real? You ain't kidding?" Cindy inched closer.

"For real." Kathleen repeated the girl's own phrase. "Bridget worked on these orphan trains so she could take our younger brother and sister to find a home. During her trip, she met a man who is now her husband, Carl. Together, they did many trips to find homes for orphans but now they live in Riverside Springs. They are building an orphanage there."

Cindy's eyes widened and although her expression was still wary, it seemed warmer than before.

"What happened to the younger kids? Did they get to stay with your sister?"

"No Cindy, they were both adopted by the same couple. A family called Rees. They were lucky to stay together. We try to do that where possible."

Kathleen felt the girl close up. Her open expression was replaced by a look of defiance.

"Don't matter, I ain't got any brothers or sisters. Not anymore," Cindy said.

CHAPTER 21

*K*athleen took the girl's hand, but Cindy pulled it away. Kathleen didn't push it. She remained silent, waiting to see what Cindy would do next. Would she ask more questions, or would she keep quiet?

Cindy stared out the window. Without turning around she asked, "What happened to the rest of your family?"

Kathleen knew it was important to be honest, but she didn't want to scare the girl either.

"My oldest sister went away with some friends. I don't know where Maura is now, but she was an adult and a widow at the time, so old enough to make her own choices. My brothers, Shane and Michael went on an orphan train out West. It wasn't one organized by the sanctuary."

Cindy turned around, her shoulders pulled back as

if readying herself for a fight. "You trying to say the sanctuary does the best orphan trains?" Cindy asked.

"Something like that. Anyway, the boys got into trouble."

"See, I told ya. There's nothing good to come from these trains." Cindy's told you so tone made Kathleen want to react but that wouldn't be helpful to anyone. She did her best to keep her voice calm.

"No Cindy. I tried to blame the orphan train too for my brothers' problems, but the reality is they were growing wild in New York. They kept up that behavior and while what happened to them wasn't all their fault, it was partly. You can't blame other people, not all the time. Shane came back to New York, married a lady called Angel and now lives in Riverside Springs."

Cindy didn't say anything for a couple of seconds. Kathleen didn't fill the silence. If Cindy had more questions, she would ask them. Kathleen didn't have to wait long.

"If all your family lives there, how come you don't? Don't tell me it's because you love orphans so much."

Kathleen smiled. "No, it's not that. Well, not completely, although I do love my job at the sanctuary. I fell in love with a doctor I met on one of the orphan trains. He wasn't involved with the movement, just a passenger on a train. His work means he must live in New York so there you go. That's my life story.

Why don't you tell me a little about yours?" She hoped the girl would open up to her but it was too soon.

Cindy ignored the question instead asking one of her own. "You got kids?"

Taken aback, Kathleen tried to hide her reaction. Although, to be fair, she should have expected the question. "I have a son, Patrick. We adopted him when we got married."

"Don't he miss you when you are going on one of your mercy missions?"

Wincing at Cindy's cold tone, Kathleen tried to keep her voice soft. "Patrick is almost an adult. We all adopted each other if you like. He will become a doctor and is much too busy volunteering at the hospital or studying to notice whether I am there."

Cindy didn't look convinced, but that was the truth. It was part of the reason she felt so lonely and questioned the meaning of her life. Why couldn't she and Richard have a child?

"You don't want to know about my life," Cindy said. "It ain't all roses and it don't get to have a happy ending."

CHAPTER 22

*K*athleen did her best to hide the pity she felt for Cindy, knowing the young girl wouldn't appreciate it.

"I know it hasn't been easy for you. I don't know what it is like to live on the streets personally, but I've been working with children just like you for the last ten years. I am not easily shocked."

Cindy's eyes widened as her cheeks grew red. She drew back from Kathleen. "Don't you put me in the same boat as your orphans. I didn't want to get on this train. The coppers forced me. They said I could pick between going with you and going to jail. It wasn't much of a choice."

Kathleen knew Cindy was baiting her trying to get a reaction she was used to. Cindy expected Kathleen to shout or react in a harsh way. Just like most of the adults the child had previously been in contact with. Kathleen had seen it before.

She spoke calmly ignoring Cindy's declaration. "I'm glad you came with us. What type of family would you like to find?"

Cindy stared at her, her expression veering between disbelief and a hesitant curiosity. "You mean I got a choice?"

"Yes Cindy, a small one. I can try to find you a family in a town or out in the country. There aren't any big cities out in Wyoming, well not like New York. But we stop at some larger towns."

Cindy held her head to one side as she took a few seconds to think about what Kathleen had said. Just when Kathleen decided, the girl wasn't going to answer, Cindy spoke quietly. Kathleen had to bend forward to hear her.

"I'd like to live in a town. I can find somewhere that suits if the family you give me to turn out to be mean."

Kathleen resisted the urge to promise the girl everything would work out just fine. Hopefully it would but she didn't know for a fact. Cindy would resent her lies. She decided to be as honest as possible without scaring her.

"It doesn't work like that Cindy. You can't just run away if you don't like the placement. The family you go to will have to report on your progress. I encourage all our children to write to us to tell us how things are going. What you like and don't like. If something goes wrong, and it might no matter how careful we are, we will move you to another family."

She saw Cindy withdraw, a veil of indifference falling over her eyes. Kathleen kicked herself. She should have been more reassuring.

"You mean when they find out what a brat they got and kick me out?" Cindy short but resigned tone spoke volumes. The girl didn't trust anyone. Who could blame her?

"You can behave badly if you want and see if it works. Some families who look to take our children have adopted other orphans. They know it takes time. And then..."

"Then?" Cindy leaned forward slightly.

"There are people who think children are like puppies. They believe they will get a child who behaves well all the time, who smiles and is grateful. Who never cries or wets the bed."

"I ain't going to wet the bed." Cindy reared back, giving Kathleen a dirty look.

Kathleen did her best to hide a smile. She hastened to clarify what she had said.

"I'm not talking about you. Some little ones take a while to settle with a family. There can be problems with bed wetting or tantrums in the first few weeks. Most of the time our new parents are happy to wait but sometimes...well it doesn't always work out."

"Do I got to go with who you pick, or do I get a say?" Cindy asked.

"I won't ask you to go with anyone you really don't want to go with. But before you tell yourself you will hate everyone, please give it a chance." Kathleen stood up. "I best go check on everyone."

Cindy didn't move but stared out the window. Kathleen hoped she had listened to what she had said. Cindy would be difficult to place given her age and her appearance. Even though the ladies at the sanctuary had done their best, Cindy didn't look much better than she had when she first arrived, kicking and screaming. Her hair had been shorn some time ago and was only now growing back. It was blonde and curly but given its length, at first glance Cindy looked like a boy. Add her appalling manners—eating with her mouth wide open, wiping her snotty nose on her sleeve —and she was hardly what one would call endearing. It would take a special family to see the good in this child. But there was good in her, of that Kathleen was sure. She'd seen for herself how Cindy refused to let anyone, regardless of their age or stature, pick on the younger children. One of the younger kids had been in the same gang as Cindy. Toby confided to Kathleen that Cindy had acted like a mother to the younger ones, making sure they got to eat and stepping in when anyone threatened them. That was how she'd gotten the knife marks on her arms. Some gang leader tried to teach her respect for the rules.

CHAPTER 23

*A*s Kathleen tended to the smaller children, taking them to the toilet and making sure they had something to eat, she wondered where the best setting for Cindy was. She would have more choice of families in a bigger town, but that also gave her a chance to run away. To go back to living on the streets was a fate she didn't want for any child, but particularly a girl on the cusp of womanhood.

"Miss Kathleen will you tell us a story?" a girl named Julie asked. "Pieter says he only knows German ones."

"Pieter comes from Germany and is learning to speak English. He isn't being unkind," Kathleen explained wishing she could speak a little German to make the boy feel more at home. A picture of Granny popped into her mind. Was this the foreign boy for whom she had to pick a special family?

Pieter smiled uncertainly. Kathleen wasn't sure exactly how much English the boy understood. His parents had only recently immigrated to the States. They had lived in in *Kleindeutchsland*, or Little Germany as New Yorkers called it, among the large German community so didn't see the need to learn English. They had only been in America for six months when they were killed when a trolley had hit some pedestrians. Pieter's father had pushed him out of the way, saving his life.

"How about I tell you the story of Little Women?" Kathleen asked. The children had probably never heard of the civil war story, but it was written by one of Kathleen's favorite authors and it would help the time pass by faster. "Cindy would you like to join us?'

"No thanks. I'm going to sleep."

Kathleen didn't press the girl. She had a lot to process. Instead, she sat between Pieter and Billy with Toby on her lap and started her story of Little Women.

The hours passed quickly as the children demanded she tell them the rest of the story. Her mouth grew dry, but Pieter made it his job to fill up a cup with water for her. Only when their stomachs rumbled with hunger would the children let her stop.

"You tell good stories. Like *Papi*."

"Thank you, Pieter, that's a real compliment. Do you like to read?"

"In German yes. In English, it is difficult. But I hope to learn. If I can."

Kathleen saw the boy was trying hard to be brave. She compared him to Teddy and Laurie. Although of similar age, Pieter's life couldn't be more different. Not only had he lost his parents, but he lived in a strange country where everyone spoke a different language. If only Reverend Haas had been able to find him a family in Little Germany. But times were tough. There was a lot of competition for jobs and families in that area were struggling to look after their own. Maybe she would find a German family willing to take on this lovely child.

"It is important to keep up your schooling. I will make sure your new family knows you like to read," she told him.

"Thank you, Miss Kathleen. You are great for me."

After Kathleen had fed the children with the help of the other boys and girls, she soon had all twenty in her care settled for the night. Even Cindy was asleep, or pretending to be.

Kathleen tried to get comfortable in her seat, her book on her lap. But the hard seat was hurting her back and her mind was racing. Granny Belbin had predicted a foreign child who needed a good home. Was that Pieter? And she'd mentioned a fire hurting a child. Father Nelson said the girl she'd pick up from her uncle, Mia, was a victim of fire. So if Granny had been right on those two counts, was she also right about Richard's inability to father a child? Was she destined to meet a child who would find a loving home with her and Richard on this train?

Her mind played over the children traveling with her. Pieter was the opposite of Cindy —he'd never had to fend for himself before and wouldn't last two minutes on the streets of New York. She had to find him a good family. Some would-be adopters would take one look at his strong muscles and clear skin and see not a child but a worker.

Kathleen knew all the children would be expected to help in their new homes. They would have chores to do just like most children. Her mind flew back to the stories Bella's husband had shared of growing up an orphan on a farm out West. He and Mitch had been forced to work from sunup to sundown and were treated horribly. The newspapers that highlighted the fact that some children became almost like slaves to their new families weren't always wrong. But not the kids from the sanctuary. No child in her care would end up that way. Of that she was certain.

CHAPTER 24

The train stopped at a small station the next morning. There were only two passengers standing on the platform. George, the conductor, came to find Kathleen.

"Miss Kathleen, the gentleman outside wants a word with you. Says he's been in contact with Father Nelson. I will come with you."

Pleased, if amused, by George's effort to protect her, Kathleen asked Cindy to look after the children.

"George, it's fine. Father Nelson arranged for me to collect the child."

"All the same, I will wait with you."

Kathleen stepped off the train, looking at the figures in front of her. The man aged in his early twenties looked stressed, as if being on the station platform was the last place he wanted to be. The child beside him held onto his hand, her long black hair twirling around her face with the wind.

"Mrs. Kathleen Green." Kathleen held out her hand. The man shook it but didn't offer his own name.

"Father Nelson said to give you Mia. You'd know a good home for her. I can't look after her. Lord knows I've tried, but I ain't set up for looking after children. I didn't know it would be this hard."

Horrified, Kathleen glanced at the young girl, but she hadn't appeared to hear. She was practically glued to the young man's side.

The man couldn't seem to stop talking. "I live in a small town where everyone knows everyone else. Anyway, I got to be going. You take her now. Mia, let go of my leg. You go with this lady now. She'll find you a new home. With kind people."

This added remark made Kathleen look closer at the man. Surprised to find tears in his eyes, she wondered if she had misjudged him. But her heart went out to the child holding his leg. She must have been terrified.

"Hello Mia, my name is Kathleen. I am taking a group of children to Green River. We would love you to come with us."

Mia glanced up at Kathleen just as the wind lifted her hair. The child's face was marked with a horrific red scar. Granny's words came to mind. A child hurt by fire. Granny had seen Mia. Kathleen's heart hammered so loudly, she was sure the others could hear it. Kathleen used every ounce of self-control not to move. She had to restrain herself from picking the child up in her arms and running back to the train.

Despite Kathleen's lack of reaction, the child must have expected her to cringe as she turned her face back into her uncle's leg.

Kathleen bent down to speak to Mia.

"Mia, darling, I know you are scared. We are strangers now but by the time we get to Green River, we will be friends. I have some other girls in the group, they might be the same age as you."

Mia didn't look up. She clung tighter to the young man despite his attempts to free himself.

George stepped forward. "Miss Kathleen, I don't mean to intrude but we have to get going. The train has to arrive on time at the next station or there will be upset."

"Sorry George. We're coming now. Mia, can you take my hand?" She glanced at the uncle. "Does she have anything to take with her?"

The man looked rather bemused before his neck turned red. "You mean clothes and stuff. That's all she got. I told you Missus, I is only a small farmer. I don't have money to buy stuff like that. I can't look after a kid. Look Mia, we spoke about this. You will have a better life somewhere else. Without me. I got to go now. Be happy."

The man wrenched his leg away from the child and stomped off. Mia tried to run after him, but he was too fast.

CHAPTER 25

*K*athleen moved quickly and gathered the child to her, picking her up and carrying her onto the train. She held her in her arms until she reached the car with the other children in it.

"What's wrong with her? Why's she wailing like a half drowned cat?"

"Cindy. Be kind. This is Mia. She is coming with us to Green River."

Kathleen sat on the seat with Mia on her lap, the child's face buried in her chest. The train whistled before it moved off away from the station. Glancing out the window, she saw the young man staring at the train, the tears running freely down his face. Her heart went out to him and to the child on her lap.

Billy moved closer.

"You're an orphan like me. We can be friends,"

Billy said, moving forward when Mia didn't turn her face. "How do you like..." Billy stared at Mia's face. "What did you do to your face? It looks awful sore."

Kathleen waited to see if the child would respond but when Mia stayed silent, she gently explained.

"Mia was injured in a fire. The scars will heal in time." Kathleen smiled at Billy, hoping he wouldn't cry or scream, but he seemed to accept what she'd said. The child on her lap was a different story.

"No, they won't. They will be like this forever. They said so at the hospital."

Shocked to hear Mia speaking so eloquently, Kathleen stared her in the face. Mia was watching her closely for a reaction. Kathleen thanked the Lord for her husband Richard and his work with burn victims. She had seen cases like Mia before and while the scars never ceased to upset her, she didn't run in revulsion.

"I hope the doctors are wrong, Mia. Now why don't you take a seat here beside us and tell us a bit about yourself?"

But Mia seemed to have used up her words and although she moved off Kathleen's lap, she sat in silence. Kathleen had to see to the needs of the other children so left Mia with Cindy and Billy. Billy was kindness himself, but Cindy was the one who surprised Kathleen. She spoke softly to the young girl, telling her about how they would find her a family who would love her and look after her. Kathleen knew

Cindy didn't believe that would happen for her, but maybe she believed it would happen for the little ones. Kathleen crossed her fingers. If Cindy believed good things could happen, it should be easier to convince the young girl they would happen for her as well.

ired the next morning, Kathleen rubbed her aching back. The children were fretful, having slept badly on the train.

"Morning Miss Kathleen, you don't look as if you slept well. Anything I can help with?"

"George, you don't look so rested yourself. Are you saying I look dreadful?" Kathleen pretended to be insulted, causing the older man to blush. She smiled to show she was joking. "Do you think we will stop soon to take on water? The children could do with a runabout."

"Yes, Miss Kathleen in about an hour. We have to pick up coal and a large shipment for one cattle baron. Can't afford to get on their bad side, you know."

"What did he mean by that?" one child asked as George went off about his business.

Kathleen hastened to reassure the anxious little boy.

"He was just teasing, Billy. In the old days there was a lot of trouble with ranchers in Wyoming."

The boy's eyes widened. "Like gun trouble with cowboys and all sorts? Do you think I could be a cowboy Miss Kathleen?"

"You ain't never been on a horse have ya?" Cindy responded. Mia was asleep on her lap.

Kathleen glared at the girl before she turned her attention back to Billy, now sitting crestfallen back on his seat.

"I think you would make the best cowboy Billy. You are good with animals. I heard from Father Nelson you were superb with the cats and dogs."

"Yes, Miss Kathleen I love all animals. I hope to get adopted by a farmer. Then I can see animals every day," Billy said.

"There will be plenty of farmers at the center in Green River. They are used to us stopping there and make us welcome these days. I will keep in mind your wish to live on a farm."

Billy gave her a hug. She hugged him back, a little part of her feeling slightly jealous of the people who would become this little boy's parents. He was shy and nervous around other children but patient with animals. Father Nelson didn't know much about him. Billy had been found curled up asleep in a coal bunker at Father Nelson's house. All inquiries had led nowhere with Billy himself not able to tell anyone where he came from. He had spent two years in the New York orphanage in the hope someone would come forward. Billy had been well cared for, not the usual half-starved child wearing rags that usually was abandoned. But nobody came. Kathleen knew Father Nelson had been upset saying goodbye to the sweet lad.

"Cindy, when the train stops, could you look after the younger girls and I will watch the boys?"

"I'll take the boys and Mia. They run faster and you won't be able to catch them. Not dressed like that. You should have worn something more suitable."

Amused at being given fashion advice by the younger girl, Kathleen didn't disagree with her.

"Wyoming is a good state for you to live in Cindy."

"Why?"

"They are more forward thinking than most on women's rights," Kathleen said. "A woman can vote in Wyoming, for example."

"You mean they think boys and girls are the same?" Cindy asked, her tone suggesting she didn't believe Kathleen.

Again, Kathleen was struck by the keen intelligence of the young girl. If she had been born into a family with a little money, the girl could have excelled at school.

"Not exactly, but there are more chances for women to do different jobs here."

Confusion dulled Cindy's eyes so Kathleen let the matter drop. If Lily were there, she would tease her for trying to teach a child about the suffragette movement. The children were eager to get outside. Kathleen decided to let the topic slide for now.

"Girls, don't go too far. Boys, do what Cindy says. A whistle will sound when the train is going to leave. We don't want anyone left behind."

CHAPTER 27

athleen counted the children to make sure there were all present. She didn't think anyone had stayed on board the train, but she wasn't taking any chances.

George passed her a small basket when she left the train.

"Miss Lily said I was to surprise you with this when I thought you needed a pick me up."

Tears sprung into her eyes at the man's kindness. "God bless Lily and yourself, George."

"Miss Lily is a fine woman, just like yourself. Now go on, you don't want to be wasting your time chattering away. I got a job to do."

Kathleen took the basket, and the rug she had been carrying, over to an area of fresh green grass. Mia sat beside her, obviously not in the mood for playing. One child ran up to her.

"Look Miss Kathleen, they have flowers. Can I pick some?"

"You can, just be careful not to wander far. I have a surprise for all of you." Kathleen showed the basket.

The children ran around, playing games and running races. Kathleen sat on the blanket watching them. Pieter didn't join in the games but sat by himself a little ways off. Kathleen beckoned to him to come and join her and Mia.

"What is wrong Pieter, why don't you play with the others?"

"I listened to what you told Billy. Will I get home with farmer?"

She didn't correct his English, wanting instead to find out why he was asking. "Is that what you want?"

Pieter shook his head, his expression making it difficult for Kathleen not to give him a hug. But he was distant, and she didn't want to overwhelm him with signs of affection.

"Can I ask why?"

"Animals make my eyes cry. And make me do this." Pieter forced a sneeze. "My skin–I have to do this a lot." He scratched his arms. Afraid he would hurt himself, she took his hands.

"Pieter, it sounds like a farm would be the worst place for you to live. I will try to find you something in Green River. It is our last stop." It wasn't, Riverside Springs was, but what could the boy do in the small town? There were farmers who would take on orphans, but she couldn't think of someone in the town who could afford to take on the child. He could live with Bridget and Carl in the orphanage perhaps, but surely his chances of finding a German family were better in Green River.

"Green River," he said. "Why the water is green?"

"It's just a name of the town, that's all. Are you hungry?" she tried to distract him. When he nodded, she suggested he call the rest of the children.

"Eat time. It's eat time."

"Lunch time, Pieter."

"Oops. Sorry." Pieter called again. "Lunch time. Come quick or I will eat yours."

Kathleen smiled at the boy who once more took a seat. She had to find him something to suit him. A family with the financial ability to let him continue his schooling. There were some German families in Green River. Maybe they would be more likely to take in a child from their own country. Cindy moved closer.

"What's in the basket?"

"I don't know, Cindy. It was a surprise from Miss Lily. I thought I'd wait until everyone was ready before I opened it."

"I love surprises Miss Kathleen." Billy looked up at her, his innocent sweet smile making her want to grab him and run away.

"I do too, Billy." She opened the basket, and the children cheered. Lily had packed some cookies and some candies Cook used to make at Christmas. The old dear must have been working all night.

"Everyone take a cookie and a piece of candy and then pass it on to the next child. You don't need to take two pieces." She admonished one child, gently watching him as he put the second piece back in the box.

Kathleen took some apples out of the box as well and then she found a note address to her. She opened it and quietly read the contents.

"'Dear Kathleen, always remember their lives will be better than the ones left behind. XX.'"

She recognized Lily's handwriting. Her friend was right. Since the sanctuary had gotten involved, they had encountered very few problems. The trials Bella had been through all those years before were enough to make sure everyone involved did their jobs properly. Even now, the thoughts of what could have happened to Meg and Eileen if Bella hadn't fought so hard to protect them made Kathleen shudder.

She chased those thoughts away. It was pointless dwelling on the what ifs. Bella had not only rescued the twins but also the other children those horrible brothers had been abusing. Someone had sent them to new homes. Kathleen wondered if anyone checked up on those children in the last ten years. They hadn't come through the sanctuary so she didn't have access to those records.

CHAPTER 28

The train arrived at the next town. Again, Kathleen and the children disembarked but this time it wasn't just to stretch their legs. Kathleen hoped to find families for at least five of her orphans, maybe more. They had placed children there before and the families had spread the news about the work done by Father Nelson and the sanctuary. Two local families had written asking to adopt young boys.

She thought about getting the children changed into new clothes but this stop didn't give them enough time to have a bath. She decided it was best to just leave them be. She walked with the group toward the church where the would be parents were waiting.

"Why do they have signs up, Miss Kathleen? Are they planning a party?"

"Of sorts Pieter. The signs are to welcome you and the rest of the children. This town has taken orphans from the train before. They always welcome us with a small gathering, cakes and nice cold drinks. It is a lovely place."

Pieter's face fell and he looked at his feet.

"I will miss the party in Little Germany. Our pastor was taking us in River boat. We were going to have lots to eat. I was going with my new friend Hans and his sister, Frieda. At least they were hoping to go. They didn't have tickets. But Papi did. Papi said we would have wonderful time but then... I don't know what happened to the tickets. Maybe I could have given them to Hans and Frieda?" Pieter brushed his eye. Kathleen pretended not to see the tears.

"It sounds like it would have been a good party. Maybe we can have a small party when we get to Green River."

"You not find me home here?"

Kathleen looked around the small gathering. She knew a few of the faces.

"I don't think so Pieter. I think this town would be too small. But we will see."

He nodded, his facial expression so trusting she had a lump in her throat. She swallowed hard before turning her attention to the task in hand.

"Pastor John, another warm welcome. You truly spoil us."

"Miss Kathleen, you and your friends deserve this small gesture of appreciation. The children you give to us have brought so much joy to their families and to this community. People come together now from all over to meet in our little town. We owe you a lot."

Blushing Kathleen looked away from the warm admiration in his eyes. Bridget had told her how this man had asked after her a few years ago.

"My husband and I are very glad everything is working out so well. We hope our latest group of children will be very happy."

"Your husband is still working in New York? He should move out here and see what a wonderful life you could have. Plenty of space and no noise." Pastor John shuddered making Kathleen smile.

"Richard likes the noise but he should come out here for a vacation. Maybe he will come with me next time. Now, where are the parents you want me to meet?"

It didn't take long to match up the two boys with their prospective parents. Another couple were interested in adopting and soon Mary-Beth had found herself a family.

CHAPTER 29

$\mathcal{K}$athleen was about to go and eat with Pastor John and the others she knew when a couple came forward. She saw them looking at Rebecca. She sent up a quick prayer they would be interested in adopting Rachel too as she didn't want the sisters to be separated if she could avoid it.

The girls, with their dark solemn eyes, had seen enough sadness to last them a life time.

"Rachel and Rebecca," said the women with interest, "what lovely names. Straight from the bible."

Rachel put her arm around Rebecca. "We are Jewish, and we wish to remain in our faith." The girl spoke confidently, but not in a disrespectful way. Kathleen was proud of the child.

The woman who'd come forward looked at Rachel approvingly.

"Yes, this is good as we are of the same faith. Your parents would be proud."

"Our mother died because of our religion. Papa," Rachel paused as her voice quivered, "he made me promise to keep the faith. As a testament to him."

"Your mother was killed in New York? In America?" The man looked to Kathleen who immediately felt guilty even though that was silly. She didn't know of anyone killed for their religious beliefs in New York. For their wallet or their jewelry or because they walked into the wrong street, but not for their place of worship. She looked to Rachel hoping she would answer.

"No, in Russia. My father brought us from Russia to live with his brother in New York. But then he died in an accident on a building site. Our aunt, she brought us to live in the orphanage one year later."

The woman's eyes thinned. "How cruel. What type of evil woman would do that? To forsake her own family." The woman looked ready to string up the offending aunt. Kathleen hoped that was a good sign and she would offer the sisters a home.

"No, please don't think like that," Rachel said. "She was crying. She said they tried, but they didn't have the money to keep us. She asked for our forgiveness."

Kathleen bit her lip as she watched the horror on the other woman's face.

"Oh, child forgive me for jumping to conclusions. I am wicked, not your aunt. You are a very brave young girl to speak up for your family." The woman stopped, her voice breaking. Her husband put his arm around the woman's shoulders.

"What my wife is trying to say, is that we would love to welcome you to our home. We have five sons."

Kathleen looked into his eyes. Could they afford two extra mouths? The man must have sensed her next question.

"Yes, it is a lot and God is good. But my wife, she would love a daughter. And what better than a daughter but to have two?" The man smiled at Rachel and Rebecca. "I cannot take the place of your father, but I would like to be as close to you as your uncle. Would you give us a chance? We own a store. My wife is a wonderful cook. She bakes the best pastries as you can see." The man patted his expansive stomach making Rebecca laugh. Even the solemn Rachel cracked a smile. "We sell what I do not eat. Even with my size, the store is successful. God has been good to us."

What a nice kind man, joking and making the children laugh as he gave them time to process his offer. Kathleen warmed to the couple. She waited to hear what Rachel would say but the child didn't speak. She motioned her to come closer. "Is something wrong, Rachel?"

"Will they let their sons be mean to us? The boys weren't always nice in the orphanage."

Kathleen rushed to explain. "I'm afraid some of the children at the orphanage were unkind to the girls.

They didn't understand their customs and got offended when the girls wouldn't eat with them at special occasions like Christmas. We explained it was due to religious reasons and most children were fine. But there are always one or two who will pick on someone different."

The man replied, looking at Rachel. "Yes, always. Sometimes adults too, but we must treat these people with kindness. We must pray for them for only then will they come to see we Jews are not evil or wicked or Christ killers."

The woman gave her husband a dig in the arm as if to tell him to shush. "My boys will not be unkind and if they are, I will make their backsides as red as a tomato. I bring my boys up to respect women. Isn't that right Joseph Stern?"

"Hannah, please, the girl is frightened. You do not need to scare her more."

"Oh, my little petals. I do not want to scare you. I want to feed you and dress you and hug you. Please say you will come home with us."

Rebecca made the decision. She moved toward the lady and held her arms out. "Mama."

The couple stared at her, but not for the same reason as Rachel and Kathleen.

"That is the first time she has spoken since our father died. I thought she had forgotten how." Rachel rubbed a tear from her face. "Please, can we go home with you?"

"Is it allowed? We are not church people, although the pastor, he is a kind man. He said we were good parents."

"Yes Mr. Stern, you seem to make very good parents. Pastor John has vetted almost everyone here. If you fill out the necessary papers, the girls are free to go with you. Rachel would like to continue to keep in touch with her aunt."

"Why yes, of course. Perhaps we can send her some of my wife's pastries. Maybe on the train?"

Rachel's eyes lit up. Kathleen gave the girls a hug, shook Mr. Stern's hand, and was about to shake Mrs. Stern's when she was gathered into the biggest hug ever. The woman smelled of spices and baking and perhaps a little too much garlic.

"You are a special lady. God will grant you your deepest wishes. Thank you for coming to our town and bringing our girls."

Kathleen nodded, not able to speak. Lord above, but please let this day end soon. She didn't know how much longer she would be able to keep the tears at bay.

CHAPTER 30

*S*he sat on the picnic rug watching as the children who had been matched with new families got to know them. The children returning to the train with her were eating their fill and playing with the local children as if they didn't have a care in the world.

She knew the children who left New York under the care of the sanctuary or the aid agency Father Nelson was involved with, were luckier than most. Now the families were vetted by the local mayor or head of the town churches. Everyone who took a child had to sign a contract to keep in touch with the sanctuary. Those that did not do so, were followed up on as soon as possible.

If only that were the way for children from all outplacement agencies. She wished people would focus on improving the services rather than trying to stop orphan trains from landing in different communities. Father Nelson was right to worry about the changes in the law. There were now seven different states who refused to allow orphan children to settle there without a bond payment. It was supposed to make sure the children would never become a burden on the state. But what of the rights of those children?

Pastor John had taken his leave saying he had to visit some outlying farms and would travel back with the Sterns. Rachel promised to write to Kathleen and both girls gave her a hug before being whisked away by their parents. Mrs. Stern had insisted on buying every child left to return on the train a present at the local store.

Kathleen sat enjoying the sunshine waiting until George sent the signal the train would pull out. She must have dozed off as his whistle woke her up.

"Miss Kathleen, hurry. The train will leave without us. I want to find my farmer." Billy tugged at her sleeve. She brushed the hair from her eyes, wishing she had some water to wash her face. And a chance to change her dress. But there was no time and no proper facilities. She would have to wait for the hotel at Green River. The thoughts of a night's sleep in a proper bed tempted her to hurry back on the train.

"THANK YOU, Cindy, for gathering up the children.

That was kind of you to help. You are especially good with Mia."

Cindy looked surprised that someone had noticed her efforts. She opened her mouth, but instead of a retort, she muttered a thank you. Her face flushed before she walked ahead of Kathleen taking a seat in the corner of the car.

Kathleen counted and recounted the children. Fifteen left. All were full and happy to take the next step in their journey. Pieter came to stand beside her.

"Miss Kathleen, Cindy and I can mind everyone for a while. You go sleep."

"Thank you." Kathleen didn't intend to fall asleep again but soon the rocking motion of the train took effect.

CHAPTER 31

ater that afternoon, they arrived in Green River. She counted the children again, this time telling them to take their belongings with them as they left the train.

"That's it, leave nothing behind you." She helped the younger ones, relieved to see Cindy and Pieter doing the same. Cindy held Mia's hand firmly, and the child seemed to be glad. Billy didn't look as happy as before, in fact he looked terrified.

Kathleen moved to reassure him. "Billy, we won't be meeting our new families today. We will stay in a hotel where we can have a bath."

"I had a bath last Saturday. I don't need another one."

Kathleen smiled at the fierce expression on his face. What was it with little boys and baths? "Yes, you do, we all do. After all the time in the train, we don't smell so good. Now, come on. Follow me. Cindy, will you wait please till last to make sure everyone gets off?"

"Yes."

Kathleen moved slowly, not wanting to lose anyone. She couldn't believe it when she heard her name being called.

"Kathleen Green, I missed you." Next thing she knew, Bella threw her arms around her.

"Bella. I didn't know you were coming to meet the train."

"Brian and I came. Shane and Angel have the children. We wouldn't let you handle the children alone. Brian will take care of the boys and between us we can handle the girls. Oh, Kathleen I've missed you so much."

Overcome with emotion, Kathleen couldn't say a word and instead hugged her friend. Then together everyone got off the train. The children waved goodbye to George, whose eyes were suspiciously bright.

Once off the train, Kathleen saw Brian waiting for her with another surprise. Her younger brother, Liam, was standing beside Brian. She couldn't believe her eyes. He was so tall and the spitting image of Shane. She stepped forward to greet him.

"Liam, you came too?"

"Do you think I would let you come all the way from New York and not ride in to see you? I miss you telling me what to do."

Kathleen playfully slapped him on the back. He

was taller than her now. And so handsome. She hadn't seen him in over three years. Where had the time gone?

"That was Bridget not me, but it's great to see you. You are so tall and grown up looking."

"I am grown up, Kathleen. I'm not a child anymore."

She could see that was true.

"Bridget said to tell you there is a room at her house for you. They are expecting you to stay for a few days. Mary-Jane is so excited you are coming, she even promised to wear a dress for Bridget."

Kathleen laughed. She knew from Bridget's letters, her niece Mary-Jane believed she should have been born a boy. Bridget teased Carl it was his fault for announcing to the world their first and only baby would be a boy. Instead, a tiny baby had arrived a month early but with a temperament of steel. With her big blue eyes, she had wound her parents around her little finger from that first day in New York.

Tempted, Kathleen wished she could say yes. But she hadn't cleared it with Lily. Who would mind the sanctuary?

Bella seemed to read her mind.

"Bridget wired Lily and she has asked some women to help in the sanctuary. Said you were to take a few days to rest."

"You guys are conspiring behind my back," Kathleen protested, but secretly she was thrilled. She hugged Liam, trying not to feel hurt when he pushed her away.

"Kathleen, stop that. You're embarrassing me."

Bella took Kathleen's arm.

"Liam likes no one kissing him unless you happen to be a certain dark-haired young lady."

"Bella!" Liam warned.

Kathleen watched in amusement as her younger brother's ears turned red. She hadn't heard he was courting, but she didn't want to embarrass him further.

"Bella, how are things with you?" she asked to distract everyone from poor Liam.

"Great. I can't wait to catch up with all your news. But first let's get everyone to the hotel and into the bathhouse." Bella sniffed the air pretending to take offense. As Kathleen giggled, she spotted an annoyed look on Cindy's face.

"Bella, you go ahead. Mia, could you take Bella's hand? I just want a minute alone with Cindy."

Mia took the hint. She walked on with Bella, leaving Kathleen alone with Cindy.

"Cindy, Bella and I are old friends. We used to work in the sewing room at the sanctuary."

Cindy stared at Bella's back, her lips curling. "Doesn't give her the right to laugh at us."

Kathleen saw the girl was genuinely hurt. She felt awful.

"No, it doesn't, but Bella wasn't laughing at us. She

is like my sister. She was teasing us. She knows how difficult it is to travel by train. Especially as an orphan."

Cindy rolled her eyes. "How? She doesn't look like she ever knew any hard work."

"That's where looks can be deceiving. Bella rode the orphan train, not once but twice. I won't tell you her story, but it would surprise you to find out how similar you are. Don't judge people by what they look like, Cindy. Appearances are often deceptive."

Cindy looked mutinous but didn't reply. Kathleen picked up her basket, Brian having already taken her bag, and walked.

"You best hurry or you will bathe in cold water, Cindy."

The girl strode off. Kathleen wished she had found a way to reach her, but she didn't have enough time. She walked down the street, spotting Bella waiting for her at the turn. Cindy had taken control of Mia once more as the two girls walked ahead.

CHAPTER 32

"Hard trip?" Bella asked as they walked toward the hotel.

"It doesn't get any easier." Kathleen tried to be positive. "I am so glad you came to Green River."

"So am I. I miss you so much and letters aren't the same. How are Richard and Patrick?"

"Both are doing well. Richard is always busy at the hospital and now Patrick goes after school. He wants to become a doctor, so it is good practice."

Bella cocked her head to one side, but Kathleen pretended not to see. She stared ahead, determined not to talk about her problems. Compared to what these children were going through, she had none. She didn't want Bella asking questions, so she changed the topic.

"So, how are the plans for the orphanage going? Bridget wrote to say you had found some opposition to it."

Bella's eyes hardened. "You could say that. Some people in Riverside Springs thought having an orphanage would lead to an increase in crime. Honestly, you should hear some of them. I was all set to write to Lily and get her to come down and sort them out."

Kathleen could just see Lily striding into action.

"Bridget won them over in the end. She told them real-life stories of some orphans. She changed their names, but the impact was the same. Even the most hard-hearted people there came around. All except Mrs. Willis."

Kathleen didn't know who that was. "I don't remember meeting a Mrs. Willis."

"You haven't had the pleasure. She is some distant cousin of Geoff Rees. Must be very distant as they couldn't be less alike if they tried. She has some money and bought a large spread to the north of town. As you know, we want it near the new school, but she objected. Says the children from New York will taint the Riverside children."

Kathleen stopped in her stride. "That's ridiculous. Apart from anything else, does she know just how many of the Riverside children came from New York?"

"She knows. I might have told her on more than one occasion. Oh Kathleen, I don't have the temperament for dealing with the likes of Mrs. Willis. She is just so...so judgmental. Why did she have to come live in our town? It was perfect, well, near enough until that woman arrived."

Kathleen couldn't answer that.

"Does she have a family of her own?"

Bella shook her head. "No, no husband either. Just her and her mangy looking cat."

Kathleen burst out laughing but even as she did so, she thought of Granny's prediction. She had seen a lady and her black cat in the tea leaves.

"The cat isn't black is it?" Kathleen asked despite herself.

Bella stared at her. "Yes it is, how did you know? Has Bridget written to you about Mrs. Willis?"

Granny had got something else right. Kathleen pushed the thought away.

"Bella. You can't blame the cat for her owner."

"Just wait till you meet this cat. I swear it's her shadow—is that what you call it when someone comes back in cat form?"

Kathleen laughed again. Bella soon joined in. "Sorry, she just drives me up the walls."

"Bella, you can't come back as anything if you are not dead." At Bella's puzzled look, Kathleen explained. "You said Mrs. Willis is alive and well."

Bella quickly retorted. "Miracles could happen, maybe she will do the decent thing and disappear while we are here in Green River."

"Bella Curran, you can't go around saying things like that. If Father Nelson was here, he would give you a dozen prayers to say for your soul." Kathleen linked her arm with her friend, thrilled to have her close. She'd missed her so much.

"If Father Nelson was here, he would get rid of that woman and her cat. Brian will tell you. The both of them are a menace."

athleen didn't get to find out anything more about Mrs. Willis as they arrived at the hotel. Everyone was waiting for her. The boys and girls were chattering among themselves. She clapped her hands to get their attention.

"Children listen please. Boys, you go with Brian and he will help you get situated. Girls, follow me and Bella. We will all meet back down here at five for dinner."

"Yes, Mrs. Green." The chorus of voices caught the attention of other guests. Some smiled toward the children, but many had a less kind reaction. A couple sniffed the air. Kathleen could see Bella's temper rising so she stepped in quickly.

"Right come along, children. I can't wait to see you all in your new clothes."

Her words had the right effect as the children

hurried upstairs. Kathleen gave Brian a bag of boy's clothes. "Good luck."

"Thanks Kathleen, but how hard can it be? I have two boys now."

Kathleen didn't tell him dealing with eight tired boys would be rather different. He could find that out for himself.

Bella escorted half the girls to one room, while Cindy and the remaining girls followed Kathleen.

"Can we keep the clothes we have?" a girl asked, her hand in the pocket of the outfit she'd worn on the train. In the old days, they had changed the children into new clothes before they left New York. But a few trips and experience with the smoke-filled train cars made them come up with a different plan. Now the children washed and changed once they arrived at the town in which they hoped to be placed.

"No dear. Best we don't. You all have two new full sets of clothes."

Cindy took a step back. "I ain't giving up my dress. You can't make me. They tried to take it away before. All that happened was they tore it."

Looking at the torn dress which barely covered the tips of her ankles and stretched too tight across the bodice, Kathleen was tempted to argue. But she held her tongue. The dress was all that Cindy owned, and it was understandable she would want to keep it.

"We can wash it and see if those marks come

out. In the meantime, have your bath and we will see how your new clothes look."

Cindy didn't look convinced, but at least she didn't argue. Kathleen considered the girl for two seconds before becoming engrossed in seeing to the needs of the others. She and Cindy were the same height. Cindy was much thinner, but it still might work. One of the dresses she had brought with her would suit Cindy's coloring. It was prettier than the orphanage clothes. She would need Bella's help to get it taken in, but maybe she could put a smile on the girl's face. Feeling happier, she turned to the younger girls and was soon up to her elbows in suds.

CHAPTER 34

*O*nce they were all washed and dressed in their new clothes, Kathleen helped the girls with their hair. Cindy turned out to be an accomplished hairdresser, completing five sets of braids while Kathleen was still on the first child. Mia wouldn't let them put her hair in braids. Cindy didn't push her.

"Where did you get so good at doing braids?" Bella asked Cindy.

Cindy didn't bother to look at Bella but responded rudely, "In the orphanage. Where do you think?"

"Cindy, don't be rude," Kathleen admonished her. "Bella was only asking."

"Well, I hardly learnt how to do braids in a salon on Fifth Avenue, did I?"

"Cindy. That's enough. Apologize please."

"Sorry." Cindy was out the door before Kathleen

could stop her. She went to go after her, but Bella said to leave her be.

"Poor girl, she's probably terrified and too proud to show it. I remember how she feels. What type of family have you picked for her?" Bella asked.

Kathleen finished the braid she was working on, in silence.

"Kathleen?"

"I haven't any picked out for her. Father Molloy had a letter from one couple asking for a girl Cindy's age to help on their farm. He thought it would be a good match."

"But you don't?" Bella questioned.

"She would be wasted in that position," Kathleen retorted.

Kathleen continued to take her time braiding hair, but she should have known Bella wouldn't leave it at that. Bella sat forward in her chair.

"Why do I get a bad feeling about this?"

"It's not because of anything bad," Kathleen assured her. "Cindy is a clever girl. I think being stuck on a farm would be the worst placement. I wish I had an alternative."

Bella sighed. "You had me worried. I thought you had found out something bad about the people who applied for Cindy to come live with them. There might be an alternative."

Kathleen eyed Bella curiously.

"What about taking her to Riverside Springs?

You've seen how good she is with the children. She could help Bridget. And with the new master in town to teach the older children, she could stay on at school. Then she could become a teacher like Angel did or something else. A pharmacist even."

Bemused, Kathleen stared at Bella who rolled her eyes.

"Kathleen, haven't you read about Cora Dow in your papers? They had an article on her in one Carl gave me to read. She is a qualified pharmacist, but even more surprising she now owns something like ten of her own drug stores. She has an ice cream factory too. Things are changing, Kathleen."

"I never thought you were a suffragette, I thought that was Lily's thing. You always seemed to be so happy being a wife and mother," Kathleen said.

Bella pretended to be horrified. She put her hands over her mouth as if Kathleen had cursed.

"Kathleen Green! Do you not remember I set up my own dressmaking business? You were supposed to come with me. We were going to take over the world."

Kathleen giggled. "Yes, I remember. But then you met Brian and, well, the rest is history."

She wondered if Bella's idea would work. What would Cindy think about it? She couldn't believe the girl would relish attending school with its accompanying rules, but she could ask her. She could at least give the girl some control over her future.

"Miss Kathleen, my belly hurts. Can we feed it?" Mia asked, reminding Kathleen of her presence.

Bella and Kathleen exchanged a look again, but they tried to subdue their giggles. Now was the time to act their age, not behave like a couple of school girls.

"Yes of course we can. Let's go downstairs and show everyone how pretty you look," Bella said.

Kathleen watched the little girl's smile widen in response to Bella's compliment. The young girl twirled in her new clothes. Even though it was a plain pinafore, it was probably the nicest thing the child had ever owned. Kathleen's eyes filed up. Lord above, but she was becoming way too sentimental in her old age.

CHAPTER 35

The next day, it was time to take the orphans to the church hall to meet their prospective parents. Kathleen hadn't had a chance to speak to Cindy privately. The night before the girl had avoided her by going to bed early, possibly as she thought Kathleen might be angry at her rudeness to Bella. This morning, some of the younger children were complaining of bellyaches. Kathleen knew they were nervous as they clung to her. Mia clung to Cindy. She tried to reassure everyone, grateful Bella and Brian were also on hand. Liam took Pieter under his wing and the two of them were getting along famously.

"Bella, I need to speak to Cindy. Could you take Mia and the younger ones, and I will follow you in a few minutes."

"Of course. Good luck." Bella whisked the little ones out of the room so fast they didn't get a chance to cry for Kathleen. Cindy started for the door, but Kathleen was too quick for her.

"Cindy, I'd like to speak with you."

Cindy glared at her, her arms folded across her chest. "Are you going to tell me off?"

"No, although I was hurt by your rudeness to my friend. I have an idea I would like to discuss with you. Sit down please."

Cindy sat on the very edge of the bed, her arms still crossed. Kathleen knew she had to be gentle.

"I was wondering how you felt about not getting a placement today?"

"You think nobody would want a brat like me?" The girl looked defiant, but Kathleen could tell it was partly an act.

"No Cindy, I don't think that at all. Lots of families would love to have you stay with them. You are wonderful with children."

"You mean they want a slave," Cindy said. "An unpaid worker."

The girl was trying her patience.

"Cindy, please stop. I am trying to help you."

"You are? Why? Why do you keep singling me out? Do you feel sorry for me or something? Cause I am telling ya now I am fine. I don't need nobody."

"That's not true, we all need somebody. We need someone to believe in us. I think you are a very bright young woman and, if given the chance, you could become anything you want. An attorney or maybe a doctor, a teacher or a pharmacist."

"I don't know what that even means," Cindy said. "But I think you must be drinking. Look at me. I ain't never going to amount to nothing more than I am. A New York street rat."

Kathleen shook her head.

"You can be anything you want. You were born with a good brain. All you need to do is get a hold on that temper, change your attitude and the world could be at your feet."

Cindy glared at Kathleen. "You think it's so simple don't ya?" Cindy stood up. "It's easy for you in your fancy dresses, lording it above the likes of us. Makes you feel good coming on the orphan trains to give us poor kids a chance. I don't need your sympathy Missus, or your silly notions. I'll find my own family. Thanks for nothing."

Kathleen didn't know who was more shocked, herself or Cindy, when she pushed the child back down on the bed.

"Sit down and shut up. Listen to me. You have a brain and you are worth so much more than what you believe. I told you before, I used to live in the tenements. But for Bridget, my sister, myself and Liam and the rest of our siblings would have been on the streets. Just like you. Now I got something for you. Can you sit there long enough for me to get it?"

Cindy didn't say a word, but she didn't move

either. Kathleen walked over to the door and took the dress she had been hiding off the hook.

"This is for you. Bella and I, made this for you."

Cindy reached out to touch the dress, but her fingers lingered an inch from it, as if she was afraid to touch it.

"For me? I ain't never seen anything so pretty."

"Why don't you try it on?" Kathleen prompted.

"Now?"

"Yes, but hurry. I can't miss the start of the meeting. I'm supposed to introduce the children to the townsfolk."

CHAPTER 36

*C*indy stripped off her clothes, but she took her time putting the new dress on. She couldn't do the back up. She turned to Kathleen asking shyly, "Could you help me. Please?"

Kathleen tried to hide her joy at Cindy's reaction. She didn't want the younger girl to retreat behind the devil may care attitude she usually adopted.

"Of course." Kathleen did up the buttons. Then she looked over Cindy's shoulder into the reflection in the mirror. "You look beautiful."

Cindy didn't speak. She stared at herself, as if not believing it was her in the mirror.

"Don't you like it?" Kathleen asked.

Before Kathleen could react, Cindy turned and buried her head in Kathleen's shoulder. The tears wet through her dress.

"Cindy darling, take it off if you don't like it. I

didn't want to upset you. We thought you would like it. Please don't cry." Tears dropped down Kathleen's cheeks too. "Please."

"I love it." Cindy hiccupped. "I ain't never had nobody give me something of my own. That dress I wouldn't give you. I stole it. Off a clothes line. I know I shouldn't have, but I wanted something pretty. I saw it there, fluttering in the wind and had to have it."

Kathleen drew the girl closer, pushing the hair back from her eyes. "I understand that feeling. Honest, I do."

"What did you want to tell me?"

"I wanted to ask you something, not tell you. I wondered if you would like to come with me to Riverside Springs to meet Bridget. My sister needs help, but she won't admit it. She has a weak heart. I worry she is taking on too much with the orphanage she has planned."

"You thought I would work in it."

"Yes, but not the way you think. I thought you could help her in the mornings and after school."

Cindy took a step back. "School? That's for young uns."

"Actually, it isn't. Most children finish school long before they should. They have to, as their families need them to work and help pay for food and stuff. But with an education you can do anything. Be anyone. Look at my husband. He's a doctor. He wasn't born rich." Kathleen crossed her fingers. Richard's family might not have been as rich as he was now, but they hadn't exactly been living anywhere near Hell's Kitchen. Cindy didn't need to know that.

"You really believe I could go to school? I ain't been near one since I was little. Not since..."

"Since?" Kathleen pushed.

"Ma died. Then the woman where ma lived said I had to take her place or get out. Ma made me swear I wouldn't do what she'd done. She couldn't help it. She got me in her belly and my dad, well he..." Cindy was blushing and looking everywhere but at Kathleen.

Kathleen put her finger under Cindy's chin and gently forced her to make eye contact. "He left your mother alone and pregnant."

"Pretty much. She couldn't go back to her family. They didn't want her. So, she did the only thing she knew. But she was a good ma. She was kind and made me laugh. You know, she had a lovely smile. Well, before the sickness got her."

"Cindy, your mother sounds like a wonderful lady," Kathleen said.

Cindy's eyes sparked. "You just saying that aren't ya. You type of people don't believe a woman that sells her body could be good."

Kathleen thought back to what little she knew of Lily's background. She was the best woman Kathleen knew.

"I don't think what you do to survive has anything to do with the person you are. I really believe that,

Cindy. But we both know if you stay on the streets or go to the wrong house, you could end up in the same situation as your mother. You are very pretty and sometimes that can attract the wrong attention."

"But it wouldn't in Riverside Springs?" Cindy asked.

Cindy's knowledgeable tone made Kathleen wince. When would the day come when twelve-year-olds were protected from the worst of life? "It might, but there would be people there to protect you. It is a wonderful little town, but it has its share of problems. Nowhere is perfect. But the key question is, are you willing to give it a chance?"

Cindy was silent for a while. Kathleen tried her best not to move, despite wanting to flee out the door and see how the other children were doing. She needed to be in two places as the same time, but this was the most important.

She felt Cindy's hand slide into hers.

"I can't promise to be good in school. I don't know much, but I do know my letters and I can do some math. Ma taught me."

"I think you will do your mother proud. Now, why don't you dry your eyes and let's go down and see how the others are faring shall we?"

Cindy nodded. She looked at the dress once more. "Should I take it off? I might get it dirty."

"It doesn't matter, we can wash it. But you can't go

running off in it. A lady never runs." Kathleen smiled to show Cindy she wasn't giving her a lecture.

"Now I understand why. They wouldn't get very far in this get up, would they?" Cindy smiled—the first real smile Kathleen had seen from the girl. She hoped this was the start of a new friendship for both of them.

As they walked toward the church hall in silence, Cindy was the first to speak.

"I will apologize to your friend when I see her." Cindy didn't turn her face but continued to stare at the street in front of her. Kathleen knew it had taken a lot for her to say what she had.

"Bella will be a good friend to you too, Cindy."

Cindy shrugged her shoulders, but Kathleen didn't push the point. In time, Cindy would hopefully learn to trust others. But for now, she needed to learn to believe in herself.

hen they arrived at the church hall, the local priest was giving a talk.

"He couldn't resist a captive audience. Thank goodness you came," Bella hissed as Kathleen walked toward the front of the hall. She apologized for keeping people waiting due to a last-minute change of plan. She watched as Cindy spoke to Bella and, judging by the smile on her friend's face, she could tell Cindy had apologized.

Kathleen moved toward the center of the stage.

"Father Matthew, Mayor, ladies and gentlemen, thank you all so much for coming to meet our children today. As you can see, they are all well behaved and looking forward to their new homes. Why don't I introduce you to them?"

"Why don't you sit down and stop jabbering, Missus. We can see them. What more do we need? My missus wants a girl to help her in the house and a boy to work on the farm. Those two will do just nicely."

The man walked up to the front of the stage and put his hand on Pieter's shoulder. Pieter winced, but before Kathleen could move, Brian stepped forward.

"Take a step back mister, before you leave this building. This isn't a cattle auction. Have you given your details to Father Matthew?"

Kathleen was glad Brian asked this question. The man didn't look like someone she would entrust a child too. Not only did he have mean eyes, but he kept spitting streams of tobacco out the side of his mouth.

The man didn't stop chewing. "You take your turn, stranger."

"I'm not here to adopt a child," Brian replied.

"Then shut up and go home. I got what I came for. You and you come on now. There's chores to be done."

Before Kathleen could intervene, Brian picked the man up. Being twice his size, it wasn't difficult for him.

Liam stepped forward. "Need a hand, Brian?"

"Yes son, could you open the door so I can throw this filth out where he belongs?"

The crowd gasped, but nobody stood forward to come to the man's defense. Even his wife seemed to melt back into her seat as if ashamed of his behavior.

"You let me down. I'll get the sheriff on you."

"Tell him Brian Curran said hi. Now go on, get. Next time you think of putting a hand on a child, you just think of my face."

The man didn't get a chance to respond.

Liam shut the door as Brian returned to Kathleen's side.

"Thank you," she whispered out the side of her mouth. Then, moving toward Pieter who was shaking, she took his hand and pushed him toward Bella. "Take him back to the hotel, please. Cindy, will you help Bella?"

Kathleen needed Cindy out of the way or otherwise Mia wouldn't have a chance of being placed.

Cindy nodded. Giving Mia a kiss on her good cheek, she spoke quietly to her before moving to the front of the stage. Taking Pieter's arm, she walked him out of the church hall like it was something she did every day of the week. Bella followed with one last look at Kathleen. Kathleen was glad Brian was with her. And Liam. They wouldn't let anything happen to her or any of the children.

a woman came forward, her husband following close behind. "Excuse me missus, but I was wondering if I, I mean we, could speak to that cute little boy over there. He has such a lovely smile."

"Of course," Kathleen said. "His name is Billy. Billy, come here please."

Billy came running up to them. "Do you have a farm?"

The woman was a little taken aback. "Why yes, we do."

"Sold. Take me," Billy said. "I will be a very good worker. But can I play with the animals when my chores are done?"

The woman looked at Kathleen, uncertainty written all over her face. Kathleen bent down to speak to Billy.

"Billy, darling I told you before. You aren't here to

be anyone's worker. We want a family to look after you and bring you up."

Billy didn't look too convinced. The woman moved closer.

"God didn't bless me with children. I want a son. You even look like my Jeremiah, don't he, missus?"

Kathleen wasn't sure who Jeremiah was for a moment until the woman linked arms with her husband. She tried to think of the right words. What resemblance could the lady possibly see between the skinny looking man with few teeth and Billy's wide-eyed innocence.

"What happened to his parents?" the woman asked.

Kathleen gestured to Liam to take Billy back to the other children for a few minutes. She didn't want the child to overhear the conversation.

"We aren't sure, ma'am. Billy was found fast asleep in the coal cellar of our local priest. We believe he was wandering the streets alone. Well dressed and obviously cared for, but alone. He lived at the orphanage for a while but it's a been over two years and nobody has claimed him."

The woman took a hanky out of her bag and sniffled.

"Oh, the poor boy. Who could do that to their own child?"

Kathleen was quick to correct her perception.

"We don't think his parents deserted him by

choice. We, at least the police and Father Nelson think it may have been an accident."

"The police?" The woman glanced nervously at her husband.

Kathleen kicked herself. Weren't the papers full of horror stories telling the public that New York orphans would bring the police to their door? Or the local sheriff.

"Ma'am, we wanted to check that Billy's parents weren't looking for him. Billy is as innocent as the day is long."

"The little angel." The woman beamed in the direction of Billy who was happily playing with Liam.

"Why don't you tell me something about yourself, Mrs..." Kathleen didn't know the lady's name. If only she had taken the sheet of would-be families from Father Mathew. But being late had made her disorganized.

"Higgins. Wilma and Ted Higgins. We've never been blessed with children of our own. Just thought that was God's way. But then our neighbors, they adopted the two cutest little girls from one of your orphan trains. They are as happy as can be. So, me and Ted, we got to speaking. Why can't we do the same? We got a nice place, not too big but not too small neither. We don't want a worker, we got some men who work for us. We want a boy to raise as our son."

To her horror, Kathleen wanted just for a second to find a reason not to let Billy go with this couple. She wanted to keep him for herself, if she were honest. But that wasn't the way things were done. Billy wanted to live on a farm and these people seemed to be well suited to give him a very good life.

"Billy is a lovely little boy and, as you saw, is mad about animals. He has a natural gift with them. He is very eager to please." Kathleen stopped to consider how to phrase the next point as gently as possible. "Billy will have to write to us on a regular basis to tell us how he is getting on."

"Quite right, too. Don't you hear such horrible stories about what happens to the dear children? We couldn't imagine anyone hurting a child could we, Ted?"

Ted didn't respond. Kathleen guessed Wilma spoke for both of them quite a lot of the time.

"We will have him write to you every Sunday. After church. That be okay?"

Kathleen nodded.

Then Ted found his voice. "But what about his parents? If he ain't an orphan, he can't be our son. We best find another one, Wilma."

Wilma turned on her husband.

"Don't you go saying that about my son, Ted Higgins. I told you God would show me the one and that's the one he chooses. I want Billy."

"But Wilma..."

"But Wilma nothing. He ain't got parents, didn't you hear the lady? She said nobody came to find him in a whole two years. Can't help thinking if he was well cared for and then they suddenly found him on the streets, his parents likely met with an accident or some such. Anyway, we need a son and he need a home. Right missus?"

Kathleen knew better than to get involved between husband and wife.

"Why don't you take Billy over to that table and have a chat with him? I will come by in a little while to answer any questions you might have."

Before she had the words out of her mouth, Wilma had gone to claim Billy.

"I don't mean to sound nasty, missus. I wouldn't want to see the boy left with a man like your fella threw out. But I can't bear my Wilma to hurt. It took her so long to accept she wasn't going to have children. She told me I ought to leave her and go find another woman. But I told her she be right stupid. I married her and I'm going to stay married to her. She be the best wife any man could wish for and then some."

Kathleen swallowed hard. Now she could see why Wilma thought Billy resembled her husband. So much for her telling Cindy not to judge people by appearances. Hadn't she just done the same?

"Thank you, Mr. Higgins. I assure you we believe the parents to be dead. Either way, after all this time it is highly unlikely, they would come looking for Billy. We could have placed him with a family before now, but we were hoping to reunite him with his parents.

He doesn't have any memories of them or at least he hasn't spoken of them."

The man tipped his hat at her and then went to find his wife.

Kathleen had to take a deep breath to get a hold on her emotions. She wondered if Richard would defend her quite so fiercely. If she offered to leave him so he could find another wife to give him a child, would he decline so vigorously?

Liam moved to her side.

"Sis, you alright? You look very pale. Want me to fetch Bella back?"

"No, thank you, Liam, but I appreciate your thoughtfulness." Kathleen squeezed her brother's arm affectionately before turning her attention back to her charges.

The hours passed and they were able to match up most of the remaining children, not always with as loving homes as they had found for Billy. But at least the orphans would have a chance at a decent life and be fed and housed.

CHAPTER 39

She was left with three children, excluding Pieter and Cindy. She walked back to the stage where the little group waited. Liam was playing with two of the boys. They had rolled up a sweater into a makeshift football and were messing around. Mia sat on her own fiddling with her hair.

"Hello sweetheart, you did well today." Kathleen took a seat next to the child.

"Nobody wanted me," the girl said.

"They don't know you," Kathleen replied, desperately trying to find the words to console the girl. She knew why people didn't adopt Mia. The kind ones would worry that they didn't have the money for further treatment if her burns needed medical help. The less generous ones would worry what their neighbors thought of this child with half of her face was covered in a red raised burn mark.

"My parents didn't want me. I'll never find a family." The girl put her head on Kathleen's shoulder.

"Sweetheart, who told you that about your parents? Father Nelson told me they probably died in the fire."

"You don't know that for sure. Stephen told me the truth. My mother screamed when she saw me, and my father died of fright."

"Mia, you forget that nonsense at once. Wait till I get my hands on Stephen. That's a horrible thing to say, and it isn't the truth." Kathleen knew the boy Mia mentioned. He wasn't one of the sanctuary children but a long-term project of Father Nelson's. Everyone else saw Stephen for the mean-spirited bully he was, but Father Nelson was convinced there was good in him, somewhere. Inspector Griffin didn't share Father Nelson's feelings. The policeman had left Kathleen in no doubt he believed Stephen would end up in the tombs, the notorious New York prison, and what's more, it was where he belonged.

Father Nelson believed every child could be saved, something the rest of those involved with the sanctuary didn't believe. As Mini Mike said, some were born evil, and that was the way it was.

"So why did they leave me?" Mia's whispered question got Kathleen's attention.

Kathleen gathered the girl onto her lap. "They didn't leave you, or at least not the way you think. We believe they may have died in the same fire you got hurt in. You don't remember and we have no way to find out. You were found at the hospital."

Kathleen hoped that would be enough information, but the younger girl had more questions.

"Did they dump me because of the way I look?"

"No. Whoever brought you to the hospital, saved your life. You'd have died otherwise. I am sure your parents loved you. Any parents would."

Kathleen wished she could tell the child she wanted to adopt her. But she couldn't. She had to speak to Richard first. She knew he would probably agree. But still, it wasn't up to her alone. The worst thing she could do was to build up Mia's hopes only to have them dashed.

Why hadn't she told Richard about her visit to Granny Belbin and the old lady's prediction Kathleen would find a child who needed a home? What better father could Mia hope for? A father who could help repair the damage done by the fire. It was fate that had thrown them together.

Mia tried to speak but it took a couple of attempts before she found her voice.

"Not unless they were blind." Mia's eyes lit up. "Maybe you could take me somewhere blind people live and then they would be my mother. It wouldn't matter they couldn't see me."

"Oh Mia," Kathleen cuddled the girl close as the tears came. She cried too. For the harsh world they

187

lived in which wouldn't give a chance to this little girl. She seemed so sweet and kind.

"Come on, Mia darling, let's get out of here and go back to the hotel. You can have a bath if you like?"

Mia hiccuped as she put a hand toward her face. Kathleen tried to stop her from scratching. She knew from what Richard said, that burns could become very itchy but if scratched there was a risk of infection.

"Mia, don't touch your face, sweetheart. You could hurt yourself."

As Mia pulled her hand away, Kathleen glimpsed the back of her neck. The scars weren't confined to her face, but usually the ones on her body were pale compared to her face. Today they looked red and angry. Kathleen felt the child's forehead. She felt a little hot. But it was very warm inside.

"I saw a store that sold cream-sodas on our way here. Would you like one?"

"Oh yes, please. The nurses at the hospital used to sneak ice-cream in to me sometimes. They were kind. I miss it there." The tears formed again but only in one eye. Kathleen had missed that the first time. The eye on the damaged side of her face didn't cry.

"Right, let's grab my brother Liam who, despite telling me he is all grown up, loves ice-cream. We can buy one for Toby and Finn too. And then we will find out what Cindy and Pieter were doing all this time."

"Miss Kathleen?"

"Yes, Mia."

"Are you going to take me to live in the orphanage? The one your sister has?"

"I don't know yet," Kathleen answered carefully. "Would you like that?"

She was surprised when Mia shook her head.

"Why sweetheart? My sister is kind."

"Yes, but children aren't. They make fun of me. I'd like to go back to New York. To the hospital." Mia shuddered before her voice broke on the last word, "Please."

Mia flung herself at Kathleen again. She didn't have the heart to tell the child that avenue was closed. The hospital Mia had stayed in had exhausted all avenues of treatment. But maybe Richard could help?

CHAPTER 40

*O*nce they got back to the hotel, Bella took one look at Kathleen and sent her upstairs to her room for a nap. She sent Cindy up a couple of minutes later with a cup of tea and instructions that Kathleen was not to reappear downstairs until later that evening. They would stay one more night in the hotel and then head to Riverside Springs the next day. Brian was paying and Kathleen was to relax.

But she couldn't. Every time she closed her eyes, she saw Mia and then Granny Belbin and the look on her face over the tea leaves. She must have fallen asleep as she woke herself up by screaming out. She'd dreamt Richard was calling for her but couldn't reach her. She was losing her mind. Frightened out of her wits, she got up and dressed. Just as she was putting the final touches to her hair, she heard the soft knock on the door.

"Kathleen, Mia is crying for you," Cindy said from the other side. "Can I bring her in?"

"Of course."

Cindy came in holding Mia's hand. As soon as she saw Kathleen the young child ran to her.

"What happened? Why is she so upset?"

"Liam took the boys outside to play ball. We went out to watch and then two boys and girls, locals, came over. They weren't nice to anyone, but they were unkind to Mia. They called her horrible names."

"I'm a monster. I want to go home. Please take me back to the hospital. At least there they have other people who look like me. Please, Miss Kathleen, you can make it happen. Please."

CHAPTER 41

athleen thought long and hard over the journey to Riverside Springs arguing with herself over whether she should tell Mia of her plans to adopt her. She sat beside the child in the back of Brian's wagon. Liam entertained Toby and Finn while Kathleen nursed Mia. The girl had a fever, but it wasn't too high. They all hoped it was just the torment of the last few days.

Soon they reached the center of town where Bridget's daughter Mary-Jane was waiting for them. Or rather, she was halfway up a tree screaming hello. Bridget came running out of the new building with Angel behind her.

"Kathleen, so good to see you. Children welcome. You must all be parched. There is some lemonade on the table. Mary-Jane will you take them inside."

Cindy jumped down from the wagon taking Pieter's hand.

"Yes Ma." Mary-Jane led the way, and the boys followed. Mia moved closer to Kathleen .

"It's all right, Mia. You can stay with me. This is my sister, Bridget, and my sister-in-law, Angel. They both live here in Riverside Springs now, but they came from New York. This is Mia."

"Afternoon Mia. Glad to have you with us. Do you mind if I give Kathleen a hug? I haven't seen her in such a long time." Angel stepped forward closely followed by Bridget.

"Angel, where is Shane?" Kathleen asked.

"He took the boys fishing. They were driving us mad asking when you would be coming." Angel's whole face lit up when talking about her children. "They got it into their head, Lily's twins would come with you."

"Not this time," Kathleen replied. But Teddy is dead keen to come. So, Bridget, how are the plans for the orphanage going?"

"Slowly! I thought as soon as the building was up the pace would quicken, but one after another thing has gone wrong. Nothing major, but it's slowing us down."

Kathleen didn't like seeing her sister look so troubled.

"Bella mentioned you had trouble with a certain lady," Kathleen said.

"I wouldn't call her a lady," Bridget hissed before saying loudly, "Good afternoon, Mrs. Willis. Isn't it a lovely day?"

"It was until your orphans turned up. So, this is the first batch you are going to impose on us."

Kathleen immediately disliked the woman without even seeing her. Her scathing tone reminded her of certain members of Father Nelson's church. Those who felt being poor or orphaned was a choice.

Taking a deep breath to settle her swirling stomach, Kathleen turned to look at the speaker as keeping her back to the woman would be rude. Mrs. Willis was holding a baby in her arms. No wait, it wasn't a child. Kathleen's eyes focused on the biggest cat she had ever seen. The poor animal was so overweight, her rolls had rolls. The woman's skinny hand caressed the cat, the contrast only serving to highlight the suffering of the abused animal. How could anyone claim to love animals and mistreat a pet so badly?

She sensed she was being scrutinized. Lifting her head, her gaze locked with that of the older woman. Kathleen anchored her feet to the ground despite the temptation to take a step back from the unbridled hate spewing out from the woman. What had happened to this lady to make her hate people she had never met?

"You must be the do-gooder sister. You bear a passing resemblance to Mrs. Watson. Who is the waif at your side? What sob story does she bring to our town? Why is she hiding her face? Covered in scabs and other unmentionables, I assume?"

Mia turned her head into Kathleen's dress. She could feel the little girl shaking. Fury threatened to take over Kathleen's body. She clenched her fists, her fingernails digging into the palm of her hands. She wouldn't dignify this woman by interacting with her, nor would she give Mrs. Willis the satisfaction of losing her temper. Instead, she employed the voice she used when dealing with Richard's wealthier patients. Those who expected her to have been born on the best side of town.

"Please excuse me, Mia isn't feeling too well. I best take her inside."

Kathleen took Mia's hand and walked away leaving the woman staring after her. Angel followed her inside.

"Kathleen, you did a wonderful job not losing your temper with that horrible woman. I have to get away or I will slap that awful woman. The things she says. Honestly, your priest should pray for her. And for us. One of us will murder her."

"Someone should take that poor cat away from her. She is feeding it to death."

"Victoria? Yes I suppose she is. I don't care about that animal, she's as vicious as her owner. Scratched some of the children in my class. If I had my way, I would stuff it."

"Angel!"

Kathleen laughed. Angel may have grown from the 14-year-old kid she had met back in New York, but she hadn't lost her spark or her ability to talk fast.

"Now Mia, what can I get for you?" Angel bent and spoke to the child, holding her gaze. Kathleen felt a swell of pride for the woman who had married her brother.

Mia looked up at Kathleen.

"Go on Mia. You can have anything you want," Kathleen assured her.

"Can I have some lemonade please? I'm thirsty."

"You can," Angel said, smiling. "Come to the kitchen. Kathleen, do you want to find your room upstairs? Second door from the top. Bridget got it ready for you yesterday."

Kathleen needed a few minutes alone. She was still shaking after her encounter and didn't want to upset Mia.

"Mia, I will be right down just as soon as I change. You will be fine with Angel, but Cindy is here too."

"She is, but she's on the swing out in the garden," Angel said. "Look Mia."

Bella came in the door as they looked out to see Cindy lifting her skirts almost up to her drawers as she laughed and played on the swing. Kathleen thought she had never heard a nicer sound. Cindy looked younger than her years.

"Kathleen, looks like we need to teach her how to

wear her new dress not just sew it for her," Bella said, trying to keep a straight face, but she gave up. They all laughed. The children were safe, out of the eye of the public and they needed to let off some steam. Who cared if the twelve-year-old wasn't behaving in a suitable fashion? She could learn manners in time.

CHAPTER 42

Kathleen left Mia giggling downstairs, relieved that the girl must be feeling better. She walked upstairs but hadn't reached the top when Bella came to find her.

"Now you have met the horrible Mrs. Willis. You handled her so well, I think she was secretly impressed."

"Bella, she is lucky I didn't push her over on her backside. What horrors turned her into such a hateful woman?"

"Trust you to be kind enough to think something horrible happened to her. I think she was born nasty. Anyway, enough about Mrs. Willis. I know you are tired, but I have to get back to my place now. I will see you later. I just wanted you to know I will be back. There is something bothering you, Kathleen, and I aim to find out exactly what it is," Bella promised.

"I'm fine," Kathleen told her. "Just tired."

"Yeah, tell that to someone who will believe you. You are tired, but you are not fine. Why don't you take a nap while the children are busy downstairs? They're safe here. Bridget won't let Mrs. Willis over the step."

"Oh, I missed you Bella." Kathleen gave her friend a hug and then went to her room. She didn't bother to undress but threw herself on the covers. Being around her family especially her nephews and nieces made the wish for a child even stronger. Finally she let the tears fall, soaking the pillow as she muffled the noise of her sobs. She must have cried herself to sleep. Someone, probably Bridget had come into the room at some point because when Kathleen woke, the covers from the bed were lying over her.

CHAPTER 43

*I*t was late in the evening when Kathleen went back downstairs. The children had been fed and put to bed with Cindy taking responsibility for Mia.

"Kathleen, you look so much better," Bridget said before filling the kettle and placing it on the stove. "Sit down and have a chat with me. Bella said she would come back tomorrow morning, so it is only the two of us."

"Where's Cindy ?"

"Mia wanted her to stay with her, so she did. Wonderful young girl, isn't she?"

"She is, although she is rough around the edges." Kathleen told Bridget her plans for Cindy. "She is so intelligent, Bridget. She would enjoy going to school. She is superb with the little ones too."

"I see that. Is that why you said you wanted her to

live at the orphanage rather than be adopted?" Bridget asked.

"It depends on you, really. You and Carl know Riverside Springs best. I just feel it would be a huge waste if she were to settle into a job, get married and have children. Not that it wouldn't be a good life, it would be. But she could be so much more."

"Are you sure Kathleen? I would have expected this from Lily, but you sound like a suffragette."

Kathleen knew Bridget was teasing, but it still stung a little. "Things are changing. Women have more chances now. You don't have to become a seamstress or a teacher."

"You loved being a seamstress."

"It isn't about me," Kathleen retorted sharply.

"Isn't it? What's wrong love?" Bridget came to sit beside her. "Tell me. Are you and Richard having problems?"

Kathleen shook her head, trying not to cry.

"Well, what is it then? Lily wrote to say you were working yourself into the ground. She tried to stop you going to the sanctuary so often, but you got involved at the hospital and the orphanage. You never take a break. Why?"

"I think Richard will divorce me," Kathleen said.

"Richard Green? Kathleen, the man adores you. Anyone can see that."

"You just asked me if we were having problems."

"I thought you might want to leave him." Bridget

took a second before she spoke. "You seem to be throwing yourself into other projects. I thought you might be avoiding him."

"No, it's my head I'm trying to avoid. I want a baby. I want a baby so bad and it is taking over my life."

Bridget put an arm around her as Kathleen sobbed. She heard the door opening but closing quickly again. It was just her and Bridget, her older sister.

"Sweetheart, I know exactly how you feel," Bridget said. "Maybe it will happen in time. Look how long we had to wait for Mary-Jane."

"Yes, but we've been married longer now, and nothing has happened. Richard should marry someone who can give him children."

"Of all the rubbish I ever heard, I never thought you would think something so ridiculous. It could be Richard who can't have children. It could be both of you. Or maybe God has decided not to give you a child of your own as there are so many that need your help. Lord above, Kathleen Collins how long have you been thinking this way?"

Kathleen ignored her sister using her maiden name. It was a sign Bridget was worried.

"A while."

"Kathleen, I am so sorry. If you told me you were unhappy, I would have come to New York."

"Bridget. You have a life of your own. A husband, Kenny, Mary-Jane and this place. As well as your heart problems."

"Kathleen, you're my sister. I understand more than most what you are going through. Lily would too. She was married five years or more before she had the twins. The worst thing you can do when you want a baby is to tire yourself out. You and Richard need to take a few days' vacation time and try to relax."

"He's always so busy. I feel guilty asking him to go away with me," Kathleen said.

"He would love to spend time alone with you. Have you considered he might be keeping busy because you are never home? Maybe he is having some doubts about you. Does he know how much you love him?"

Kathleen couldn't believe her ears. "Of course he does."

"Really? Have you told him?"

CHAPTER 44

Kathleen didn't answer. She couldn't remember the last time she had spent any time alone with Richard. Patrick usually had dinner with them but if he wasn't around, then Lily and Charlie or Father Nelson or some of Richard's friends would dine with them.

"You think maybe I have a point?" Bridget asked.

"We haven't been together much lately. We haven't talked in a long time. Not about anything important, that is. I guess we have grown a little apart." Kathleen didn't want to think about how long it had been since they had spent any significant time alone.

"It's nothing that can't be fixed," Bridget reassured her. "I think all married couples are guilty of this. We are so busy catching up with the stuff we have to get done, we forget to relax and enjoy all we have achieved."

Kathleen poked Bridget. "Now you sound like Father Nelson."

"I do, don't I? Maybe I need to get out as well. Lily wrote about your trip to Coney Island. Was it horrible?"

"To see the tenement fires. Yes, awful, but we were the only ones who seemed to think so. Charlie says it's because people need to see real life heroes in action. But when there are children like Mia around to show just how devastating a fire can be, why would you want to visit one in an amusement park?"

"According to the papers, it's the most popular attraction. Maybe Charlie is right, they like to see a happy ending. Poor Mia, she seems like a sweet girl. She told me today that you were taking her back to New York to live in the hospital."

Kathleen shook her head.

"No, I can't. I explained that to her, but she isn't listening. Poor child think's it's the only place she will be safe. The children are unkind, but they can be forgiven. It's the adults who stare. I want to slap them and tell them to stop it."

Bridget nodded in agreement. "Adults are always the worst. Mrs. Willis being a prime example."

"Bella told me about her but meeting her was still a shock. She is about as nasty as they come. And that cat. Someone should take it away from her, she is obviously overfeeding it"

Bridget rolled her eyes. "Yes, she is a major thorn in

my side. She hates orphans of any description, but has a particular lack of love for those from the streets of New York. I do not understand why. She seems to think we are all murderers or thieves or something."

"Maybe because everyone she meets wants to kill her?" Kathleen tried to joke but Bridget didn't smile. "She can't hurt you, can she?"

"Not me, personally, but she can hurt the progress of our orphanage and schools. We want to have a happy home here in Riverside Springs. We love it here. Our neighbors are wonderful...most of them. But she is making so much noise, some people are blaming the orphanage for causing problems. Not her."

Kathleen could see Bridget was extremely worried but she didn't know how to allay her fears. She wasn't going to tell her sister to ignore the woman. Bridget would have tried that already and it clearly hadn't worked. Kathleen wondered how Lily would deal with Mrs. Willis and her cat?

She looked up just as Bridget yawned.

"You're tired, sis. Things always look worse at night. We will find a way to deal with Mrs. Willis. We have dealt with worse things."

Bridget nodded but the expression on her face suggested she didn't hold out much hope.

It's late, shall we go to bed?" Bridget asked.

Kathleen wasn't tired but she knew Bridget was. "You go on up. I want to read for a while. And have a cup of tea since you never got around to making one."

"Oh sorry. I am such a bad hostess."

"But a wonderful sister. Thank you, Bridget. Goodnight."

"Sweet dreams."

Bridget left as Kathleen put the kettle back on to boil. She quickly made a pot of tea and sat down at the table. Rather than read, she sat thinking about what Bridget had said and also about Mia. What if Richard could help the young girl? Even if he couldn't, they were wealthy enough to give her some protection. They could hire a governess for her, so she didn't have to go to school. Would she be happy with them? But then would keeping her away from people really help Mia?

CHAPTER 45

The next morning, Bella and Angel arrived at Bridget's home. They sat around the table with Bridget and Kathleen, all discussing the children.

"Pieter would benefit from a German family," Kathleen said. "I didn't know if you have any families here looking for a child? He is not good with animals as they make him cry and sneeze. His skin gets itchy. So, a family based in town would be best."

The other women looked at each other before Angel answered. "There is nobody here who comes to mind. But I can help him with his English. Yiddish is similar to German. He seems like a nice boy."

"He is, and he's smart. I think he will be a doctor or an attorney when he grows up."

"Kathleen thinks everyone will be a doctor. Must be Richard's influence on her." Bella smiled to show she was joking. "Will he live here with you then, Bridget?"

"Yes. Him and the younger two boys. We can continue to look for suitable placements but, in the meantime, they can go to school. Cindy will also stay here. We had a good chat early this morning while Kathleen slept in."

Everyone laughed as Kathleen gave her sister a look. "You told me to sleep."

"I know I did honey, I was just teasing you. Cindy is a pure New York girl. She's brash and thorny, but underneath she appears to have a heart of gold. She is great with Mia and a godsend with the boys. I think she will settle in well."

Kathleen agreed and couldn't help feeling relieved. She was sure Cindy would blossom under the care of these wonderful women. Bella knew the issues Cindy had dealt with and maybe in time they would grow close.

"Kathleen when do you go back to New York?"

"Angel, she just arrived," Bridget responded. "Anyone would think you were trying to get rid of her."

"No, I wasn't. I was just wondering how long she would be here. Oh, I didn't mean it like that." Angel turned bright red as the others laughed.

"I have to see Meg and Eileen. Bridget said they had a surprise for me, but she won't tell me what it was."

"Oh yes, you must. The girls have been so excited

about you coming here. And Geoff and Carolyn want you to go to dinner to see them. Annie can't wait."

Kathleen nodded, dying to see her younger sibling again. "I will go back to New York on Monday if someone can drive me to Green River. Or I could get the stage."

"Nonsense." Bella said. The expression on her face warned Kathleen not to argue. "Brian will drive you. He has to get some materials anyway for the new barn he wants to build. Though what is wrong with the old one, I don't know. He says it's too small. It wouldn't be that small if he cleared out some junk he's collected."

Angel nodded in agreement. "Shane's the same. He won't throw anything out for fear we could use it next year. We haven't used it in the last five years but next year it will suddenly be needed. What are men like? They say us women keep things cluttered but in reality, it is them."

Kathleen listened to her friends chat. She loved them so much and missed them, but after her chat with Bridget, she wanted to get home to New York. She needed to speak to Richard.

"So, Kathleen, Lily mentioned you've been to see Granny Belbin. How is she?" Bella asked.

"How are the tea leaves you mean? My sister has lost her mind. Kathleen, I can't believe you had your leaves read. Does Father Nelson know? Was he mad?" Bridget asked.

Kathleen's cheeks heated even though they were

teasing her. "I don't really want to talk about it. She scared me. That was enough. I will never look at the bottom of a tea cup in the same way again."

"I don't know. I think it's fun. According to this, Shane will do all the housework and give me a day to read." Angel pretended to read from the cup. "Brian will take his two boys, little Rosie and my children off on a picnic and let myself and Bella sit around all day doing nothing. Carl will bake some cakes and feed us."

"Angel stop. You will make me cry," Bridget begged as they all laughed as Angel's predictions became more outrageous.

"It says here Mrs. Willis will fly off on her broomstick, never to be seen again."

"Now we know reading tea leaves is pointless," Bella announced. They all turned to look at her. With a straight face she continued, "There is no way Mrs. Willis and that cat would fit on a broomstick."

Kathleen thought she would be sick from laughing. How good it was to get together with these special women. If only Lily were there. She would enjoy it too.

Bella stood up, brushing down her dress to get rid of imaginary crumbs. "I best get back to the store. I left a sign saying I would be back in fifteen minutes. They will think I'm Irish if anyone sees how long the fifteen minutes was."

Kathleen smiled. Bella was always teasing her and Bridget over their Irish timekeeping or the fact they said something was just down the street when they meant it was about ten blocks away.

"Take care, Bella. I will be down to see your store later. Bridget says you are worked off your feet."

"Well, if you ever want to come and live here, I could always do with some help. Angel, are you coming?"

"Yes, I best get back to school and make sure the place hasn't burnt down," Angel said. "I have lessons to mark too."

"I forgot today is a school day. But you're not teaching?" Kathleen asked.

"No. I asked the new master to take my class too. I told him I had an urgent meeting about the orphanage. He is a very nice man, but I don't want to try his patience with my class."

CHAPTER 46

Kathleen followed Bridget into the kitchen after Bella and Angel had left. She looked around her taking everything in. Her sister made a good housewife, every counter was clean with all the utensils put away neatly. She watched as Bridget filled up the kettle and put it on the stove.

"Thank you for talking sense into me last night," Kathleen told her sister. "I see I have made things worse by not talking to Richard about my worries."

"We all make silly decisions sometimes. It's natural. Now, do you want to help me make dinner?" Bridget asked. She looked directly at Kathleen, a concerned look in her eyes. "Or would you like to go spend some time with the children?"

"I would like to talk to Mia. Do you mind?" Kathleen didn't want to offend Bridget.

"Not at all. Are you going to tell her you've decided to take her back to New York with you?"

Shocked, Kathleen stared at Bridget for a few seconds.

"How did you know that?" she asked. She thought she had been careful to hide her feelings.

"I watched you with her, Kathleen. You need that little girl as much as she needs you. Just like me with Kenny. I never regretted my decision, and even though I have Mary-Jane, I consider both of them equally to be my children."

Kathleen smiled. She knew her sister meant every word. "Where is Kenny? I didn't see him last night either."

"He works out with Geoff Rees. He wants to earn some money to go traveling."

At her sister's thinned mouth, Kathleen sat down.

"Tell me."

"Oh, Kathleen I don't know what has got into him. He says he wants to travel the world. He is going to join a ship and sail to England and from there he wants to go to Ireland and then on to Europe. He says he has dreamed about doing this and now is the time. I think he's too young."

"What does Carl say?"

"He agrees with me, but Kenny is fighting back so much, we are both terrified if we don't say yes, he will go anyway."

"Does Kenny know you are worried about that happening?" Kathleen asked.

"No, I don't think so. We haven't put it into words. I know he is a young man, but he is just sixteen. That seems rather young to be traveling alone."

"You weren't that much older when you became responsible for all of us, Bridget."

"True, but Kenny has been so sheltered here in Riverside Springs. It's not like living somewhere like New York."

"What about a compromise?" Kathleen suggested. "Send him to live with us for a year and then if he still wants to travel, he can."

"With you and Richard?"

"Yes, why not? He can be company for Patrick, they get on very well and Lily's twins would love having an older boy around. Think about it. Discuss it with Carl, and Kenny I guess."

"I will," Bridget said, looking hopeful. "Right, now go and find Mia and let me get on with dinner."

CHAPTER 47

Kathleen took Mia to the store. She sent a telegram to Richard telling him she would be home next week. She asked if he could meet her from the train. She told Mia she would introduce her to a special doctor who may help her. She didn't mention her thoughts about adoption. She should speak to her husband first before making a decision that big.

That done, they found the twins back at Bridget's house. They'd grown too impatient waiting for Kathleen to call on them.

"Ma and Pa are taking us back to New York for a visit. We will see Coney Island and the new subway and all the other places you mention in your letters. Isn't that exciting?"

Kathleen agreed that it was. The big surprise the twins had planned was a welcome dinner and dance to be held in her honor on the Saturday night. Meg showed Kathleen the dresses Bella had designed for them and confided that Eileen was courting.

"That's wonderful, Meg. What about you? Anyone catch your eye?"

"No, there's no-one around here I like. I think I shall find my prince in New York. It sounds so amazing."

Bridget grinned at Kathleen. "I think you should bring her back to Mrs. Fleming's where we met so she can see for herself exactly how unglamorous it is."

Meg rolled her eyes. "I remember. I wasn't that young when we left Mrs. Fleming. I mean when she died, and we had to go away. I want to do what you do, Kathleen. I want to work on the orphan trains. Do you think Lily would give me a job in the sanctuary until I learn the ropes?"

"She would Meg, but only with your parents' permission. Aren't you a little young?"

Meg gave her a look. "I'm almost sixteen. Girls my age are fixing on getting married."

Kathleen could tell the girl was struggling with being almost but not quite grown up. "Well, they might think about it, but I dare say most parents want them to be a little older when taking their vows."

"Kathleen, please. This little town is so small. Nothing ever happens here."

"I will talk to your parents and to Lily but in the

meantime, you should remember a good education and behaving like a lady will help your case."

Meg turned pink. "Did you see me showing Cindy how to climb the tree?"

"I did. And I reckon you're lucky Mrs. Willis didn't see you or your parents would be shocked."

Meg's cheeks grew pinker still. "I know I shouldn't, but some days I just want to be a boy. They have so much more fun."

Kathleen looked at Bridget and had to bite her lip. She didn't disagree with Meg but now wasn't the time to tell her.

CHAPTER 48

*K*athleen walked along the river, thinking about everything that had happened since she'd had Granny Belbin read her tea leaves. Granny's predictions had come true, well most of them. She had met the foreign boy and the girl hurt by fire. She had even met the woman and her cat. Mrs. Willis was every bit as bad as Granny had predicted. She was a real thorn in Bridget's side. Bridget had shared a couple of things Mrs. Willis had done. They included writing to the Bishop and telling him the children weren't attending a Catholic church. She had also written to various newspapers giving false reports of children being used as slaves on the nearby farms. She had somehow heard of Meg and Eileen's near disastrous experience and had reframed that to make it sound like Carl and Bridget had knowingly placed the children in harms way.

Bridget was right to be worried. Mrs. Willis could easily close down the Riverside Springs orphanage before it got a chance to get up and running.

Screams intruded on her thoughts. They were coming from a wooded area nearby. Without a thought for her safety, she pulled up her skirts and started to run. She heard Pieter telling someone to stay still. She slowed down for fear of making the situation worse. Her niece came bursting through the trees.

"Mary-Jane, what's wrong? Why are you screaming?"

"Aunty Kathleen, Mrs. Willis came at us out of nowhere. We didn't see her, honest. She was about to hit us with her stick when she tripped over something. There's a wolf."

Kathleen couldn't believe her ears. Wolves didn't attack, at least not on their own. Was there a pack nearby? She would have heard if they had been attacking farm animals or sheep.

"Calm down Mary-Jane, you are speaking too fast. Breathe slowly." She held her niece's hand. The young girl was shaking. Kathleen pulled her close, but the girl couldn't stop.

"There's a wolf. Mrs. Willis is hurt and can't move. Pieter told me to go for help."

Kathleen's heart stilled as the hairs on the back of her neck stood up. "Where is Pieter now?"

"He stayed with Mrs. Willis. She told him to go

away. She was really mean, but he just ignored her. He was throwing rocks at the wolf. I have to get help."

"Who else was with you?" Kathleen asked, her heart racing so hard she thought it would come through her chest.

"Some of the boys but they took off at the sight of Mrs. Willis."

Hopefully they had gone back to town to get help.

"Mary-Jane, go to the nearest farm and get help. Tell them to bring guns and get someone to follow with a wagon. Find your mother and get the doctor. Go on now."

"But what about you?"

"I will be fine. Go, run as fast as you can. Good girl."

She waited for her niece to take off and then turned back to the woods. Looking around her she picked up a large piece of wood. She couldn't leave Pieter alone. Nor Mrs. Willis. Especially if she was hurt.

CHAPTER 49

"*G*e Weg. Go away. Shoo."

Kathleen heard Pieter shouting in German and English. She moved slowly as carefully as possible trying not to make a sound even though she knew it was dumb. Wolves had a highly trained sense of smell and hearing, didn't they? What did she know?

Then she saw it. A fierce animal baring its teeth and growling. But not moving. She saw Pieter, standing tall, a stick in his hands. Behind him, Mrs. Willis was on the ground, her eyes stuck on the beast.

"Pieter, move away slowly." Kathleen was glad her voice sounded confident even though she was terrified.

"No."

Kathleen looked around but thankfully there were no signs of any other wolves. She glanced at the wolf again, it wasn't a he but a she and a new mother if she was any judge of animals. The wolf looked a bit like one of the old cats back in the tenement. Maybe her babies were nearby and that was why she was growling. She didn't look to be starving.

"Pieter, I will stay with Mrs. Willis. You need to move away." Kathleen moved closer, the wolf sensing her presence and growling. She didn't know if she was making the situation worse but she had to get Pieter away from the animal. If the wolf attacked, the little boy wouldn't stand a chance.

"Sorry. No leave. Man protect women. *Papi* say so." Pieter stood taller. Mrs. Willis whimpered.

"Mrs. Willis, how badly are you hurt?" Kathleen asked.

"I think my ankle is twisted but I don't care about that. Victoria is missing. The boys must have taken her."

Victoria? Her cat. The woman was complaining about her cat.

"Pieter didn't take Victoria. Animals make him itch. So forget about your cat and see can you get out of that hole. I think the wolf has pups nearby. She's protecting them."

Kathleen hoped Mary-Jane had reached the nearest farm by now. "Pieter, please move back one step."

The wolf's growls grew louder. Her pups must be somewhere behind the boy. Kathleen swallowed the lump in her throat. She had to save the boy. "Pieter, don't move back. Move toward me."

Pieter glanced at her as if he thought she was mad. Maybe she was. By asking the boy to move toward her, he would come closer to the wolf. But hopefully it also meant he would be putting distance between him and the pups. Kathleen prayed she was right.

"Pieter, move one step. Now another."

The boy moved at her command. The wolf kept her teeth bared but didn't growl as furiously as before.

Kathleen took off her shawl. She moved closer to Mrs. Willis, all the time keeping her eyes trained on the wolf. "Pieter keep moving. I need you to keep moving. I will go to Mrs. Willis. When you get far enough away, run for help."

"I stay."

"No. You go. Do what I say." Kathleen hoped her command would work.

The boy looked from her to Mrs. Willis and back.

"I did not take your cat. She is not here."

CHAPTER 50

*M*rs. Willis didn't acknowledge Pieter's comment. Kathleen gave her a dirty look but spoke calmly to Pieter.

"Pieter, I hear someone coming. Move now."

Pieter followed her instructions and just as he did, Kathleen pulled him toward her for a quick second and then shoved him behind her.

"Good boy. Now go slowly until I tell you to run."

Tears trickled down his face as he hesitated. Kathleen had to convince him to move. "Pieter, this is what your *Papi* would want."

He nodded slightly before moving slowly backwards away from her. Kathleen turned her attention back to the animal, looking at the wolf more closely. She was hurt – blood running freely from a cut on her back. That was why she hadn't attacked, she probably knew she was weak.

"Mrs. Willis. I am coming to help you get out of that hole. Please do not move or say a word. I don't want to spook the wolf."

Mrs. Willis for once did as she was told. Kathleen took another step and another but the wolf had had enough. She bared her teeth and growled a warning. Torn between helping Mrs. Willis and putting them both in more danger, Kathleen hesitated.

"You stop right there, miss. Don't move. I got a clear shot."

"No!" Kathleen uttered the word before thinking. "Don't kill her. She's hurt and has pups nearby. She is only protecting them like any mother would."

"Listen lady, you can't treat wild animals like children. Now do as I say and keep still."

The shot rang out before Kathleen could argue. The wolf fell to her side.

Kathleen hurried toward Mrs. Willis who was shrieking with terror.

"Don't move please, you will only do more damage to your leg. I'm here."

But Mrs. Willis continued to thrash about, her wailing intensifying.

"I could shoot her too if it would help?" the man suggested.

Tempting as the suggestion was, Kathleen took the next best action. She swung her palm out and caught Mrs. Willis straight across the face. The sound of the slap rang through the trees. Mrs. Willis fell silent.

Kathleen glanced at her. "Sorry about that but I had to get your attention. Now let's see what you did to your leg."

Kathleen ignored the woman's outraged expression and bent to examine the leg. "You're lucky. I don't think it is broken although I could be wrong. We will know more once that swelling has gone down."

"You struck me."

"Yes, and I will do it again in a heartbeat. If you hadn't accused innocent children of stealing your precious cat, you wouldn't be lying here. Pieter, that so called unwanted orphan, protected you. That child who has already seen more tragedy than he ever needs to see, could have saved your life today. Did you for one second think of the ten year old boy and how he was feeling? No you didn't. Did you know he watched his mother and father die in front of him? Yes, he did. And yet he stayed by your side until help came."

Mrs. Willis opened her mouth but Kathleen wasn't done. She continued speaking knowing if she didn't, she would never tell this woman what she thought of her. "All you can do is scream over a twisted ankle. You selfish old battle axe. You make me sick."

Kathleen turned and walked away. She marched past the farmer holding his gun.

Without looking at him, Kathleen snarled, "If she screams again, shoot her. If she stays silent, someone will be along in a few minutes to take her back to town."

"Sure things, missus. Say, you aren't figuring on settling down around here are ya? Could do with a woman like you."

athleen didn't answer. She just kept walking taking her anger out on the ground under her feet. How dare that woman put her precious Pieter in danger? Over a mangy old cat.

She spotted Bridget driving a wagon, coming toward her. Mary-Jane was beside her. There was no sign of Pieter.

"Kathleen are you all right? Mary-Jane said there was a wolf."

"The wolf is dead. Some farmer shot him. Mrs. Willis has a swollen ankle. She needs a lift back to town. Have you seen Pieter?"

Bridget shook her head. Soon more of the towns-folk arrived. "The doctor is out of town but I brought some bandages and a splint."

"Good thinking Angel. Have you seen Pieter?" Kathleen asked her sister in law.

"Yes. He was heading toward the river. I called out to him but I don't think he heard me."

Kathleen picked up her skirts and started to run in the direction Angel had pointed. The ground was too rough for a wagon to cover.

"Pieter. Where are you? Pieter?"

She found him sitting by the river in a world of his own. Moving slowly she made her way to his side.

"I was looking for you."

"You are angry?"

"No Pieter. I was worried about you. You were very brave."

"Not really. I left you and Mrs. Willis."

"I told you to do that." Kathleen moved closer but didn't touch him. His shoulders were hunched up, his arms crossed with his hands in his armpits. Tears streaked a trail through his dirty face. "Pieter you did very well today."

Pieter didn't look at her. He was staring at some point in the distance over the river.

"I let *Mutter* die. *Papi* pushed me away. I was trying to protect *Mutti* but *Papi*, he threw me to the side."

"Oh, Pieter darling. You didn't let your mother die. You couldn't have stopped that trolley. Your father saved you as he loved you so much. He and your mother wanted a good life for you." Kathleen wasn't sure how much Pieter understood. She tried to speak slower. "Your parents came to America to have a good life. To help you have a chance. They saved you. It is a parent's job to protect their children."

Pieter rubbed his arm across his face, cleaning it with his sleeve. Kathleen spotted the blood.

"Pieter you are hurt. Let me see?"

She took his hand gently.

"It is nothing. Just a scratch."

Kathleen tore a strip from her petticoat and after wetting it from the river, cleaned his hands. He was full of scratches and his skin had started to redden. He scratched it. "See the farm makes me itch."

She smiled at his comment. "The forest, Pieter. Would you like to come back to town? I know there are some very worried people thinking about you."

"People worry about me?"

"Yes, Pieter. You are one of us now. We are your family. All of us. Bridget and her husband Carl want you to live with them just like Kenny does."

"They want me?"

"Of course, they want you. Why wouldn't they? You made your parents really proud today."

"You think they are looking down from up there and can see me?" Pieter gazed up at the sky.

Kathleen shrugged her shoulders. "I like to believe so. I think my mam and baby sister are up there looking down at me."

Pieter smiled. "Yes, they with my Papi and Mutter."

Kathleen stood and held out her hand. Pieter took it and she helped pull him to his feet. "Let's go home."

"Mrs. Willis? She is all right?"

Kathleen didn't want to think about that woman, but she nodded her head in answer to his question.

"So, Pieter, how do you think you will like having Angel, I mean Mrs. Collins as your teacher."

"I will like very much. She is really handsome."

Kathleen burst out laughing causing him to look confused.

"What? Not handsome?"

"Men are handsome. Women are pretty or beautiful."

"She is like you Miss Kathleen. Very beautiful."

Kathleen couldn't speak for the lump in her throat. She squeezed his hand tightly and then together they made their way back to town.

CHAPTER 52

Kathleen came down the stairs rubbing her wet hair with a towel. She felt better after the hot soak in the tub. Pushing open the door, she wasn't too surprised to see Bridget, Angel and Bella chatting at the table.

"Well if it isn't the woman beater." Bella's teasing remark made the others smile but Kathleen caught the wary looks in their eyes. Her family were worried about her, that much was obvious. "Before you ask, Pieter is fast asleep in bed. He had a bath and a hot meal and then Angel read him a story. He is sleeping like a baby."

"Good. He was really brave today."

"You were too Kathleen, but hitting Mrs. Willis?" Bella raised her eyebrows.

"She had it coming. I was nice. I didn't let the farmer shoot her."

"Yes, the farmer. He wants to propose marriage. I told him you were already taken but he suggested you leave Richard in New York and settle down with him. You made quite the impression, Kathleen." Bridget smiled at her, but Kathleen didn't feel like smiling. She was starting to regret hitting Mrs. Willis. What if her sister and this wonderful community ended up in more trouble?

She glanced up at her friends, "I suppose I should go and apologize to Mrs. Willis."

"For what? Knocking some sense into her? From what I hear, she could have got herself and young Pieter killed. You did us all a favor. Seems she has given up all thoughts of a life in the country. She is going back to live in New York. Brooklyn." Angel grinned. "So, she won't be too close to you."

"If she did come near, I think Lily might send her packing. Can't see her taking kindly to any woman who talks about her orphans the way Mrs. Willis does."

"I don't know Bridget, I reckon Lily might see her as a challenge. For all we know she could turn Mrs. Willis into the best fund raiser the sanctuary has ever seen." Bella glanced at Kathleen. "What do you think?"

"I think if I never hear that woman's name again, it will be too soon. Who names their cat after a dead queen of England anyway?"

"Lord above knows. All I can say is thank goodness

she is leaving Riverside Springs." Bridget held her hands on her hips. "This town isn't big enough for both of us. Now she is gone, we can get back to planning our big dance in honor of my very special sister."

CHAPTER 53

*T*he night of the dance arrived. Kathleen, as guest of honor, was told to arrive last as the children and other residents wanted to surprise her. She'd made Mia a pretty dress and was amazed when the child said she wanted to go to the party.

"Cindy says it's for you and you have been so nice, so I have to go."

Kathleen smiled at the young girl. 'Cindy says' was an almost constant refrain now. The two girls had grown closer than most sisters with Cindy being very protective of Mia.

"You don't have to Mia, if you don't want to," Kathleen told her. "You can stay home here. I can stay with you. Nobody will mind."

"Yes, they will. They said you are the main guest. I want to come. But I won't dance."

Kathleen didn't argue. When Mia saw the other

children having fun, maybe she would change her mind.

They walked into the decorated barn together. It was unrecognizable as a barn, apart from the mild scent of horses. There were ribbons and banners and seating areas set up with the band playing on a type of stage. Kathleen was pleased to see there were a couple of baskets for donations for the orphanage. People from all around came to barn dances so it might be a good time to collect some money toward the Riverside Springs Orphanage. A few people came up to shake her hand and thank her for the fact Mrs. Willis had left town. Kathleen didn't like feeling she had chased the other woman away but when Geoff Rees congratulated her, she decided it was a good thing.

"May I have this dance, Mrs. Green?"

"Why Mr. Collins," Kathleen smiled as Shane led her onto the dance floor. "You seem thrilled here. Angel is wonderful, as usual."

"She is," he agreed. "My wife is an extraordinary lady. We would both like to have a quick chat with you, if you don't mind. I know the party is for you, but we made a decision and we can't wait to tell you. It's about Mia."

Kathleen's heart lurched. She glanced at Mia who was laughing and playing with some local children. They had asked a couple of questions about her burns but then seemed to accept her. She caught Cindy looking at Mia. The girl was like a mother hen with the young girl.

"What about her?" Kathleen asked.

"Come outside and speak to us both." Shane guided her out of the barn and toward the main house where Angel was waiting.

"Did you ask her?" Angel asked, her fingers fidgeting at her neckline. Kathleen glanced from her brother to his wife and back again.

"Ask me what? You're making me nervous."

"Angel wondered if—" Shane started but he was speaking too slowly.

"What Shane is trying to say is, we were wondering if we could adopt Cindy and Mia."

"The both of them?" Kathleen stuttered, trying to buy some time.

"Yes. Cindy reminds me of myself and I really feel she would benefit a lot from having a steady home. She can help Bridget in the orphanage too, but I think it would be nice for her to be part of a real family. And Mia, she is just such a special little girl. Her and Cindy are so close and couldn't bear to be parted. They are both terrified you will take Mia back to New York."

"They are?" Kathleen tried not to sound hurt. She thought Mia wanted to go with her.

"Yes, but they didn't want to tell you as they were afraid you would be angry. I explained to them you wanted the best for both. You were only taking Mia back to see Richard in case he could do something for her burns. We could still do that. Or Richard could bring you here on a holiday and you could catch up with all of us. What do you think?"

Kathleen couldn't speak.

"We have enough money if you are worried about that," Shane said. "I am doing well with the horses. I have a natural ability, according to Geoff. Angel is working and Cindy can help us with the younger ones. Please say yes, Kathleen. We really want to do this."

Kathleen looked at their faces. How could she say no to two people she loved? "What about the girls? Have you spoken to them?"

"Not really. Cindy has been spending a lot of time with me," Angel said. "We've been working on her schoolwork. She is such a bright child. Mia is too, actually. You don't see Cindy unless Mia is nearby."

That was true and Kathleen had noticed it before. She knew she had tried to hide from the truth which was that Cindy and Mia had developed a strong bond. It would be cruel to split the girls up now, especially after all they had been through. With a heavy heart, she knew she had to say yes. It was the right thing for the girls and for her family whom she adored.

"Well, If the girls agree, I suppose the paperwork can be finalized quickly."

"Oh Kathleen, thank you. Can I tell the girls?" Angel asked.

Kathleen nodded as Angel picked up her skirts and

fled. Shane stayed close to Kathleen, holding her gaze as if waiting for her to say something. When she didn't, he asked,

"Am I missing something? You don't seem too pleased."

"Don't be silly. I'm happy. Finding homes for orphans is what I do, remember?" She pushed him playfully.

He looked in her face and pulled her close.

"Kathleen, you are the best sister a man could ever hope for. I feel you might have had other plans, so thank you. From the bottom of my heart."

Kathleen hugged him back.

"Miss Kathleen, can we speak to you please?" Cindy's voice interrupted.

"Yes, Cindy."

"Thank you so much for letting me and Mia be real sisters. We are so happy, aren't we?" Cindy asked Mia.

Mia moved forward and threw her arms around Kathleen. "I love you and now you are our real aunty. Isn't that right?"

Kathleen bit her lip so hard she tasted blood. She had to be brave. She couldn't let the girls know her heart was exploding into pieces.

"Yes sweetheart. Shane will be your pa and I will be your aunt."

Mia hugged her again. "Thank you for bringing me to this special place. I love it here. People are so kind."

"You deserve every bit of happiness, Mia. You, Cindy and everyone in Riverside Springs."

Mia ran back inside and Shane soon followed. Only Cindy stayed behind.

"Will you be happy when you get home to New York?" Cindy asked.

Kathleen thought of her husband waiting for her and her stomach turned over. He was a very special man and she was lucky. Plus she had Patrick. So much to be thankful for. So what if Granny Belbin had told her a load of nonsense. "Yes, Cindy I think I will be. This trip has opened my eyes to a lot of things. My mam used to tell me when I was little, I should count my blessings. That's something I forgot to do, but you reminded me."

CHAPTER 54

Kathleen was only back in New York a couple of days when Lily invited her, Richard, and Patrick to dinner. When they arrived, they found Father Nelson and Inspector Griffin had been invited too.

Richard squeezed her hand as if to tell her it was okay for her to speak to Lily even though the others were there. When she'd returned home from her trip with the orphan train, Kathleen had asked Richard how he felt about giving an orphan a home. She'd confided how she'd wanted to adopt Mia, but although she wasn't the right child for them, meeting her had proved how much Kathleen wanted a child.

She squeezed his hand back. They were getting on so well since they had the long talk after she came back from Riverside Springs. She would speak to Lily another time. There was no rush. Bridget and Lily had been right. Richard had been concerned she wasn't happy and wanted to leave him. How silly was that? Well, just about as ridiculous as her thinking he wanted to divorce her.

"So is anyone going on the trip, Reverend Haas invited us on?" Lily asked.

"When is it again as we are very busy at the hospital" Richard glanced at Kathleen. "Sorry darling, I will try to go if you want me to."

Kathleen shook her head.

"This Wednesday June 15th." Lily confirmed the date. "We met Reverend Haas a few times when you were in Riverside Springs, Kathleen. He is a nice man."

Father Nelson nodded. "A wonderful man with a sharp mind and a gentle manner. He was instrumental in helping us to fund previous orphan trains although we didn't know it until recently. His congregation holds him in high esteem and for good reason. A more pious and charitable man you are unlikely to meet. He is about fifty years old but has the energy of most twenty-year-olds."

Kathleen hadn't met Rev. Haas, but she wasn't at all keen on going on the river on a steamboat. She was about to say so when Lily spoke up.

"I don't think I will go. I would rather the children didn't either. I know you will think I am foolish, but I don't trust those boats. Do you?" Lily looked at Inspector Griffin. He shook his head slowly.

"I don't want to diminish anyone's fun, but I

wouldn't be too keen on traveling on one either. There are still far too many accidents for my liking. There are regulations in place which are supposed to keep the boats, their owners and captains in line but rumors abound that a couple of payments in the right hands will clear any boat as being seaworthy. I prefer to keep my feet on dry land. Sorry Charlie. I don't mean to sound ungrateful."

"Not in the least." Charlie stood to pour everyone another glass of wine. "I am not sure I can make it either. My desk looks like it could collapse under the weight of the paperwork covering it. The new mayor may have underestimated the amount of work involved in curbing the corruption in the police force and elsewhere."

Kathleen glanced at Inspector Griffin. She didn't want her friend to feel uncomfortable, but he simply smiled. They had discussed the level of corruption in the past and he was one of those keen to get the police force away from the control of certain individuals in Tammany Hall. He wanted a police force that worked for the people, regardless of where those people lived or came from. He had previously spoken out about his fellow officers accepting bribes.

"What about the children, will they be very disappointed?" Richard asked Lily.

"They will, but they will have to get over it. I would rather they miss it than be in danger," Lily said.

"We can tell Rev. Haas in person tomorrow. Lily or

Kathleen, or both if you are free, would you come with me to Little Germany tomorrow? Rev. Haas would like to talk to us about some children he means to send on the orphan train. I think he would like some reassurance I won't make them become Catholics."

Everyone laughed as Father Nelson rolled his eyes. They had heard many accusations about the orphan trains but the two that seemed to stick were the taking of children from their real parents, and that it was the way of the Catholic church to find new converts.

"I'm free tomorrow," Lily said. "Are you, Kathleen?"

"Yes."

"Right then, let's meet at the church. Now enough shop talk for the time being. Cook will be very unhappy if we ruin her dinner. I better just go say goodnight to the twins. Teddy made me promise."

Hearing his mother's voice, Teddy ran up the stairs two at a time. He knew his mother would be cross if she found him listening at the door, but he wanted to go on the picnic. It sounded like great fun. Some boys in his school were going with their families. Kevin had a cousin still living near St. Mark's Church. Kevin's father was taking the day off and bringing his whole family. Kevin, with his father's permission, had asked Teddy to join them. Kevin's father had insisted Teddy get permission. Well now, he couldn't ask his parents, could he? His mom would say no, and he couldn't defy her. Not outright. But if he didn't say anything about the invitation and told his mother he would spend the day at Kevin's house, that would work. Wouldn't it?

Laurie! He could ruin everything. Teddy ran in search of his twin. He had to make sure his brother wouldn't tell their parents his plans.

CHAPTER 55

The day of the picnic dawned brightly. The sun streamed in the windows as Frieda got up and made breakfast for her siblings. She still couldn't believe they were going on the picnic. It seemed Reverend Haas had talked *Papi* into not only letting his children attend, but taking an unheard-of day off and coming with them. Reverend Haas had also arranged for Lottie to go to a special hospital. Lottie loved it and said she felt good and she could breath better.

Frieda couldn't remember the last time the family had gone anywhere together. Not even when *Mutti* was alive. She sang as she cut the brown rye bread and put the sausage on the table. *Papi* had brought home the treat last night saying they had to start the day off properly.

Soon they had eaten and were standing dressed in

their Sunday best. Due to excitement, none of them had slept well the previous night but it didn't matter. There was no sign of tiredness this morning as they got caught up in the excitement. They could hear other families getting ready through the thin walls of their tenement. Hans pulled at his collar but there was no way he would not wear it. *Papi* had insisted his family look smart and respectable. Everyone would wear their best party clothes.

Frieda cleaned off the table, leaving their rooms neat and tidy. She gathered together their food and drinks, a blanket and two towels. If *Papi* went swimming, he would have one, and she'd have to share the second one with Hans.

"Can we go now?" her brother begged. "They are all gathering in the street. I don't want to be late."

"Off you go," *Papi* said, "but don't go too far. And help your sister by carrying something."

Papi beamed at Frieda. "I am so proud of you my Frieda. You have made this day happen."

Unaccustomed to the praise, Frieda blushed. She loved her father to pieces but he wasn't the demonstrative sort. This day just couldn't get any better.

As they moved down the stairs, she bumped into Mrs. Sauer who handed her a bag of fruit.

"It won't keep long. Not in the sunshine like this, but enjoy it. I wish I was coming with you."

Feeling guilty, Frieda tried to curtail her obvious excitement. None of the Sauer family were going.

Despite Reverend Haas' best efforts, Mr. Sauer had declared he couldn't afford to take the time off. Mrs. Sauer had confided in Frieda her husband wasn't worried so much about losing trade as about the state of the steamboats. His brother was a police officer and had seen his share of accidents. His grisly stories had put an end to any chance the Sauer family had of taking part in the trip.

"I will come and see you after and tell you all about it," Frieda promised. "Thank you so much, Mrs. Sauer. You are always so kind."

"You enjoy your day Frieda. If anyone deserves it, you do."

CHAPTER 56

*A*s they walked through the thronged streets, Frieda spotted Paul Libenow, his wife Anna and their three adorable daughters. Her father had known Paul for years, long before the barman had moved his family nearer his job in Harlem.

"Paul, Anna, it is wonderful to see you. The girls are growing up so fast."

"Thanks Otto. I am so sorry about your wife and child. I meant to come back for the funeral, but I wasn't able to get the time off. Anna was pregnant with this little one," Paul said.

Frieda didn't look at her father. She wanted nothing to change his good mood, and she hoped people mentioning her mother and baby brother wouldn't do that. Judging by the crowds of people, a lot of families who had moved out of *Kleindeutchsland* had come back for the day. It was a chance not only to catch up with old friends, family and neighbors, but also to show off a little. The people who had escaped the tenements like the Libenows who had moved to the more fashionable Harlem may show off as far as Frieda was concerned. They were proof that hard work could help you achieve your dreams. Wasn't that the American promise? The reason her mother and father had emigrated in the first place.

Paul spoke again, "My sisters are here somewhere. Annie's daughter is about the same age as your Hans."

"A year older. Yes, we see them at church. Emma and Frank Jr. come with your sister and her husband. Your other sister, Martha also attends. Lovely woman she is."

Frieda saw Paul's eyes widen at *Papi's* remark. Maybe he was planning on doing some match making. Wasn't it too soon? *Mutti* hadn't been dead that long. But she knew from her experiences in Little Germany, most widowers didn't stay single for long. The older people didn't believe men could look after children, since raising a family and seeing to the household was a woman's job.

"*Papi*, I am going to see if I can help Mrs. Prawdzicki. She has five children to cope with as her husband couldn't get the day off."

"Well done Frieda, for thinking of your neighbors. Rev. Haas will be pleased to see his Sunday school lessons have paid off."

Reverend Haas didn't lead the Sunday school, but Frieda wasn't about to correct her father. She looked around for Hans, but her brother had scampered off with his friends. She wasn't worried. Hans wouldn't act badly, not with *Papi* in the vicinity. He wouldn't get lost either, not when everyone was heading the same way. Those who weren't lucky enough to be coming, were reminded by their wives to be at the pier to welcome them home. Frieda heard more than one discussion between husband and wife but all along the same lines: "Make sure to meet us at the pier on our return. You will have to carry at least one child. They will be tired after the long day."

CHAPTER 57

William Richter stood to one side as his mother ordered her brood of six children to do this and that. Frieda liked Mrs. Richter; the widow woman was a hard worker. She worked long hours as a cleaning lady, seven days a week. Reverend Haas knew she had to work on a Sunday as there was nobody else to help her keep a roof over her head and provide food for her children. Frieda glanced at William shyly, wondering if he was coming on the trip. She'd known him all her life and had always liked him. But recently, being around him made her feel different. Her hands grew clammy and sweaty. Even now she had to rub them discretely on the side of her dress.

"Morning Frieda, are you going on the trip?"

"Yes, Mrs. Richter. Can I help you with anything?" Frieda forgot she had promised to help Mary with her children.

"No need, but thank you for the offer. The older girls and I will manage. William do you have your lunch?"

"Yes *Mutti*." William's cheeks grew red as he glanced at the ground before looking up quickly. He caught her looking at him and smiled. Frieda's stomach flipped.

"You aren't coming on the trip?" she asked, her voice coming out all squeaky and making the other members of the Richter family laugh. William glared at them before turning his attention back to Frieda.

"Not today. I didn't want to risk my job. It is going well."

"That's an understatement. They love my William. Soon he will run the commission house, just you wait and see."

"*Mutti!*" William's cheeks grew a darker shade of crimson. Frieda liked that he wasn't bigheaded like a lot of the boys in the area.

"William, you must go, or you will be late. Meet us at the pier later. *Ja?*"

"Yes. I'll be there." William moved toward Frieda and said in a lower voice. "I wish I was going today. I would have offered to carry your blanket."

It was Frieda's turn for her cheeks to turn hot. "Thank you, I would have liked that."

"Maybe I can see you later. After I help *Mutti* home. We could meet on the roof and you could tell me all about it."

Frieda nodded. "I'd like that."

William beamed. "Have a great time." He kissed his mother on the cheek and strode off down the street whistling. Frieda watched until he disappeared from sight, noting his wide shoulders and tall frame. Then she caught his mother looking at her, a smile on her face.

"He is turning into a fine man, my William."

Frieda didn't know what to say in reply. Thankfully, William's mother turned back to her brood and issued orders like the best sergeant major in the US army.

Frieda hurried to catch up with her own family, all previous plans forgotten. All she could think of was William and how she was looking forward to meeting him later.

eddy got dressed and climbed out his bedroom window. He hated slipping out, but his parents had told him to stay in his room. Trust Grace to tell them about the picnic and his plans to go with Kevin. His mother had been so angry, her face went bright red. But it was his father who scared him more. He said he would use his belt the next time Teddy disobeyed him. He meant it too.

He had to take the risk and go. Picnics like this didn't happen every day. The sun was shining, and there was going to be a band and ice-cream. Someone said they might even go swimming in the river. Teddy hoped they didn't. He'd told Kevin he could swim but he couldn't. Not really. Laurie was a better swimmer than he was.

Torn between not getting into trouble and missing the fun, Teddy made his decision. He opened the window and climbed onto the roof making his way carefully to the point where the tree branch almost reached. Dad was supposed to have cut this back, but he'd forgotten. Teddy took a jump, grabbed the tree branch and climbed down to the ground. With a last look at his house, he grabbed his bicycle and off he went. If he hurried, he would meet Kevin at the pier as arranged.

* * *

Kathleen called at to Lily's house to collect Grace and Evie. She had promised them a couple of hours shopping at Macy's followed by ice-cream.

"Morning," she said as the door opened. "Are Grace and Evie ready to come shopping with me?"

"The girls are so excited, thanks Kathleen. We had a big argument last night with Teddy. He is confined to his room today. He blames Grace and called her lots of horrible names. Honestly, siblings can be truly awful to each other, can't they?"

Kathleen couldn't argue with that. Although they had been close as kids, her and Shane had argued a lot.

"Are you really going to keep Teddy in his bedroom all day? It is such a lovely summer's day. Blue skies and everything. What? Why are you laughing at me?" Kathleen asked.

"Teddy has you wrapped around his little finger,

Kathleen. If it was up to you, he would never be punished."

"Lily, I didn't mean to criticize. I'm sure you are doing what's best. But he is such an active soul. He is a mini Lily."

"Me? I wasn't as badly behaved as he was."

"Weren't you?" Kathleen smiled at her friend. "Some would say you aren't good now. Do you remember what you said to that horrible lady with the purple feathers in her hat?"

Lily put her hand to her mouth. "I guess I did go a little over the top, but she deserved it. Imagine calling my sanctuary a house of ill repute. Just because her husband would prefer to be in one of those places than at home with her and her silly hats."

"Lily Doherty. And you can't see where Teddy gets it from?"

"Oh, I suppose you are right. We were a little harsh on him. It wasn't his fault Kevin's father invited him to the Haas picnic. We should have sat Teddy down and explained why we didn't want him to go."

"Not sure telling Teddy you thought it would be dangerous would help your case much."

Lily grinned. "Guess you are right about that too. Since when did you get so wise, Mrs. Green?"

"Since I followed your example at the sanctuary, Mrs. Doherty. Now, where are the girls? We best get going and you can make it up to your son."

CHAPTER 59

*L*ily walked to the bottom of the stairs and called up to her children. "Teddy come down here and thank your aunt for getting you out of trouble again. Grace, Evie get your things, Auntie Kathleen is here to take you shopping."

Lily turned back to Kathleen. "I guess myself and Coleen will have a nice relaxing day…"

"Mom…MOM!"

Lily rolled her eyes in response to Laurie's shout.

"Laurie don't shout. Come down and tell me what's wrong," Lily answered her son before turning to Kathleen. "He probably lost his Wright brothers newspaper. I swear I don't know how it hasn't fallen to pieces. I should have told Richard to frame it when he gave to him for his birthday." Lily turned to her son, her face turning pale. "Laurie, what's wrong. Why are you upset?"

271

"Teddy isn't in his room. The window is open. His satchel is gone too."

Evie and Grace had come down the stairs behind Laurie.

"Teddy? But where would he go?" Lily mused.

Kathleen guessed immediately where Teddy had gone.

"Is Charlie here?" she asked.

"Yes, in the office."

"Laurie go get your dad and tell him to start the car. Girls, stay with Cook and we will be back shortly. Ask Cook to look after Coleen." Kathleen grabbed Lily's jacket from the hook at the back of the door. "Come on Lily."

Lily obviously wasn't thinking straight.

"But we don't know where he's gone."

"Don't we?" Kathleen asked. It took a few seconds for Lily to catch up.

"I will murder him when I get my hands on him. We told him not to go to that picnic."

Kathleen called Cook, told her quickly what happened and then bundled Lily out the door. Charlie was already waiting with the car cranked.

Lily jumped into the car, telling Charlie, "He's gone to the picnic. You will have to drive us to the pier and hope the boat hasn't gone already."

"But darling, shouldn't we just let him go? It will cause a big scene if we drive up to take him off. Teddy will be so embarrassed, and so will Kevin and his family."

Kathleen thought Charlie was right, but it wasn't her place to comment. She waited for Lily's reaction.

"I suppose you are right, but I can't help feeling he shouldn't be on that boat. Can we go to where they are having their picnic?"

"We won't be able to get to the grounds without taking a boat, Lily."

"Yes of course, how stupid of me. I just want to make sure he is there. What if he ran off and hasn't gone to the picnic? He was pretty angry with us."

"Lily darling, Teddy isn't going to run away. He has gone to the picnic. If it makes you feel better, we can check at the pier to see if the General Slocum has left and what time they expect it back. Will you come with us, Kathleen?"

Kathleen was about to suggest she would look after the children, but something told her it was better to stay with Lily. She climbed into the car and they were off.

CHAPTER 60

When they arrived at the pier, Frieda picked up a copy of the program. It was written in both German and English and gave her all the information she needed about the trip. Hans was only interested in the ice cream, which cost 5 cents, and *Papi* would enjoy a beer. She might treat them to a bowl of clam chowder at 20 cents, but first she would see what her friends and neighbors thought of the dish. She wasn't going to waste good money on bad food. *Papi* congratulated Mary Abendschein on her work, making her blush. She looked young and pretty in the early morning sun with everyone so happy around her.

Papi also greeted Rev Haas, as well as his wife and sister as they waited to climb aboard. Reverend Haas was congratulating everyone for taking the time to come to the outing as it was an important part of their parish.

Frieda glanced around her, noting that their little procession had attracted envious looks from spectators who appeared to be on their way to work or other business in the city. She hugged herself trying not to let the excitement make her squeamish. Soon they would be off.

She stared at the approaching steamer, thinking it looked like something out of a book. Smoke bellowed from the tall smokestacks, but the fresh white painted exterior dominated the horizon. The captain gave a signal and then the gangplank was lowered. First aboard were the policemen accompanying them, closely followed by Rev Haas and his family. Frieda knew most of the people climbing aboard ahead of her. Everyone was laughing and talking at the same time, the children racing ahead to see what delights were on board. The adults didn't seem to mind. They knew someone from the neighborhood would correct the children if they misbehaved. It was like one big extended family.

They took their turn waiting until it was time to board the boat and then each took their seats. *Papi* managed to secure seats together for him and Frieda, but Hans wanted to stay with his friends. *Papi* let him.

"It is nice to see him as a child for once. He has become too old for his years in recent months."

Frieda didn't argue. She rarely got her father's full attention and she was going to enjoy every minute.

They were due to depart at 8:45am, but it soon became clear they wouldn't meet that deadline.

"Look *Papi*," Frieda said. "Still they come. How is everyone going to fit?'

"Don't worry. Reverend Haas and the others know what they are doing. Nobody wants to miss today. So, what if we wait another thirty minutes? You would like us to wait for you if you were running late, yes?"

"Yes *Papi*." Frieda spoke softly as shame engulfed her. Of course, she would expect them to wait. Maybe some people had got caught in the traffic. It took about an hour before Reverend Haas was ready to go.

"*Papi*, we are going."

"Wait!" A woman stood up and gathered her children to her. "I want to get off. I have to get off."

"But, Mrs. Straub, you have paid for your tickets. The children will be so disappointed."

Frieda watched her father try to speak sense to the woman but there was no arguing with her.

"Why do you want to get off?" another man asked.

"I had nightmares about this journey last night and now my stomach won't settle. Something is wrong, I can feel it. I want to get off. Reverend Haas, let me off the boat."

Frieda watched in astonishment as the woman and her children disembarked, closely followed by the man who had questioned her. He also took his wife and children despite their tears and pleas to stay on board.

"*Papi*, do you think we should go too?"

"No Frieda. You cannot live your life on whims and feelings. I don't blame the poor woman, she is obviously exhausted looking after her children, but that man, he should have more sense. Maybe he will change his mind."

But as Frieda watched the eight disappointed children left at the pier with the three adults, she saw the decision had been made for them. The gangplank was taken up. The crew cast off. Any chance of them changing their mind and rejoining the ship had gone.

"I can't believe that woman left the boat," her father said. "Look around you. Don't you see the life preservers and the lifeboats? I don't believe anything will happen, but if her dreams did come true, they are there to stop anyone being hurt."

Frieda glanced at the life boats but didn't look closely. She didn't want to think of anything happening that could necessitate climbing into a small boat like that. She was fine in a big boat like the Slocum but anything smaller and she would get nervous. She shook her head. Papi always said it was senseless to anticipate trouble. What could go wrong on such a beautiful day?

rieda observed Reverend Haas as he made his way around the boat, chatting to children and parents alike. Then her father called her attention.

"Frieda, look at the twin paddles wheels. Those are what make the boat move. Aren't they magnificent?"

Frieda tried to feign interest, but she didn't really care how the boat moved. She watched as their friends hung over the rails of the steamboat waving to family members on the shore. It was as if they were famous or royalty or something. She waved at a man she didn't know and, to her astonishment, he waved back.

Sitting back in her seat, she put her arm though her father's and cuddled into his chest. Vibrations from deep inside the ship made it shake a little.

"Don't be alarmed, that is just the ship's engines responding to orders from the captain. When your mother and I came over by boat from the old country, you should have seen how the deck moved. We were swung from one side to the other by the large waves. But that won't happen today," he hastened to add.

Hans arrived breathless. "*Papi*, I have been playing jacks and bean ball. I'm hungry. Can I have an ice-cream?"

"Don't you have your own money, my little working boy?" *Papi* teased him as he gave Hans a few coins. The existing trace of cream around his mouth was testament to where his own money had gone. The boy disappeared. Frieda tapped her feet to the music, watching some couples dancing to the sound of the band. If William were here, maybe he would have asked her to dance.

"Frieda, you are miles away."

"Sorry *Papi*, what did you say?"

"Hans moves so quickly, it's hard to keep up with him. I need to sit him down and speak about his future."

"He is only ten." She wanted to know what he thought about her future, but she held back, not wanting to ruin the day.

"Ten is a difficult age. He could make decisions that ruin his life. By ten I was already learning the trade of my father and his father before him. It is time Hans learned how to mend shoes."

"He wants to be a news reporter," Frieda said.

"That's no career for a good German boy.

Spending all your day looking for the big story. No, he must learn his trade."

Frieda decided not to argue further. It would only upset her father and after all, Hans had a big enough mouth to use to defend himself.

CHAPTER 62

*A*s if by magic, Hans reappeared. "*Papi* there is smoke coming from a door down below."

"Yes son, it is from the engines. You will find men working down there feeding fires with coal. Of course, it will produce some smoke."

Frieda searched her father's face as he spoke. He seemed to be genuine, not just telling Hans something to stop him from panicking. Hans practically danced up and down with excitement.

"Can I see them working?" Hans asked.

"I don't know if it is allowed," *Papi* said. "You might be in their way."

"Aw please, *Papi*. I will be good and do what I am told. They won't even know I am there."

Amazed by what she saw, Frieda watched as her father ruffled her younger brother's hair. "You have a wish to find excitement in all you do. I hope your spirit soon quietens, but for today go be a child. Make sure you ask permission from the crew though."

"Yes *Papi*." Hans was off again.

"What?" Papi turned to find her staring at him.

"You are different today *Papi*. I like it."

He pulled her into a rare cuddle. "It is easy to relax, sitting in the sunshine on a beautiful day with my family beside me. You are a credit to your mother and becoming almost as beautiful. I think in no time, I will have long line of suitors coming to my door. I will have to get a shotgun."

Frieda tried to smile back but her heart hammered. What would he make of her meeting William on the roof later? Should she tell him? Ask permission? But what if he said no.

"So, Frieda, tell me about your plans. Mrs. Sauer says you still wish to pursue nursing?"

"Yes, *Papi* with all my heart."

"But why nursing? Why not teaching? It is a more honorable profession."

Frieda knew she had to be careful. Her father was old fashioned and stubborn. It would be pointless telling him about Dorothea Dix, the famous Civil War nurse or Florence Nightingale, the English heroine. But he was her father and would want her to be successful and happy, wouldn't he?

"I'd like to be a doctor," Frieda whispered her most

secret dream. To her horror, her father burst out laughing.

"A doctor. Are you suffering from the heat? No decent woman becomes a doctor. That is a man's job and a rich man's job at that."

"But *Papi*, in America women become doctors. They have done for about fifty years."

Papi pulled away from her and not just physically. She saw the light in his eyes shutter off.

"*Papi*, please just listen to me. I don't want to be a teacher or to be married young and have a houseful of children. I don't want to live in the tenements forever. I want a life."

Immediately regretting her words, she tried to apologize but didn't get a chance.

"A Life? You think we haven't given you a life? Your mother, God rest her, worked her fingers to the bone to give you a good home, nice food. She ruined her health sewing for others and for what? A child who says she wants a life. Your mother would be ashamed to have such an ungrateful daughter."

Tears pricked her eyes. "*Papi*, that's not fair. I am grateful to you for everything, but I want something more. You and *Mutti* left Germany to come here. I remember *Mutti* saying your parents weren't happy. But you still came."

"Maybe I shouldn't have," her father said. "If I had stayed in Germany, your mother would still be alive. I wouldn't be living with a daughter and son who are out of hand. I never want to hear anything about this doctor thing again. You are to put it out of your mind. Nursing too."

Frieda looked away. She couldn't agree to do that. She knew her chances of becoming a doctor were low—she didn't have the money and for all her brave words, there were few female doctors. But to give up on her dream of working in a hospital helping people? No that was something she couldn't do. She loved her father, but she was entitled to have a future of her own making. He had to listen to her. But next time, she would wait until he wasn't as tired.

But her father wasn't content with silence.

"Frieda, do you hear me? I want your word you will stop this nonsense."

"I love you. But I'm sorry, I can't give you my word. Working in a hospital means everything to me. I want to help people like Lottie. Maybe stop people like *Mutti* and baby Otto from dying."

"Tsk. You think you are God. Where are you getting these ideas from? Who is filling your head with this rubbish?"

"Please, let's just enjoy our day and forget about this for now. People are staring at us."

They were and not all of them were sympathetic toward her. She saw more than one look of disapproval from her neighbors. Still, she kept her head up. She was going to work at a hospital one way or another.

Maybe she could become a Catholic and join a nursing order. Then she pictured William's face. No, the life of a nun was not for her. But what would he think about her thoughts about her future? Would he have the same reaction as her father?

CHAPTER 63

*C*harlie turned the automobile into the pier and parked. They got out and enquired as to where they could find the General Slocum. Kathleen guessed it may be the boat she saw on the water, there seemed to be lots of people on board having a party, but she didn't say anything.

As it turned out, they only just missed the boat. It seemed Rev. Haas had waited for some stragglers.

"Look at those poor children, they must have missed the sailing." Lily pointed to some children standing on the pier.

"Nah missus, their ma took them off. They is ever so upset. But their ma kept screaming something was going to happen. She is a bit cuckoo if you ask me."

The sailor wandered off. Kathleen took in Lily's white face. "Come on Lily. Charlie, could you drive us somewhere to get a cup of tea? I think we could all benefit."

Charlie nodded. Kathleen took Lily by the arm and pulled her toward the car. The last thing her friend needed was to talk to that woman.

* * *

ON BOARD THE BOAT, Hans ran to his family.

"*Papi*," he said, breathless. "There's a fire downstairs."

"Hush Hans. You will frighten people saying things like that."

"But *Papi*, I saw it."

"Yes son, I told you before that they need to burn coal to make the steam to help the boat to move down the river."

Hans gave his father a look as if to ask how stupid he believed him to be. "*Papi*, it's not the coal bunkers but a real fire. I told the man and he didn't believe me but then he opened the door and the flames came out. He told me not to tell anyone, but I had to tell you."

Papi pulled Hans closer. "He opened the door after you told him about the smoke?"

Hans nodded.

"The stupid man. He should have kept it closed. Wasn't he taught the basics of fire safety? At the last factory I worked at, we told all our new people never to open a door if you suspect a fire."

Horrified, Frieda looked at Hans and then in the direction from where he had come. There was a little smoke for sure, but was her brother telling lies? Was he trying to create a little bit of panic because he was bored? Was he pretending to be a newspaper reporter? Her father's face was a calm mask, but she saw terror lurking in his eyes. He believed Han's story. She wanted to ask what happened next, but her voice wouldn't work. Her father spoke first.

"What did he do then?"

"He told me to go away *Papi* and I did. But..."

"But what, son?"

Embarrassed Hans looked at his feet, "I looked behind me. He threw some coal on the fire and it went out. No more flames."

Frieda noted Hans seemed a little disappointed, but whether it was over the fact the fire had gone out or the man had sent him away, she wasn't sure. Then she glanced at her father to see terror lurking in his eyes. It was gone so quickly she was convinced she imagined it.

"Frieda, try to find Reverend Haas and ask him to meet me at the top of the stairs. Don't mention anything to anyone else. We don't want to cause a panic. Hans, sit here and don't move."

"Do I have to? Can I not go back for another look?"

"Hans you will do as you are told."

"Yes *Papi*."

Hans took his seat, his legs swinging. Frieda could see how much her little brother wanted to be in the middle of the action, but he had no concept of danger. Fire was dangerous anywhere. What if it took over the boat? She pushed those thoughts from her head as she went in search of Reverend Hass.

CHAPTER 64

"Frieda don't go on the lower decks. I will search there. You stay up here and if a panic breaks out, make your way back to your brother. I will find both of you."

"Yes, *Papi*."

Surprised when he kissed the top of her head, she looked up at him.

"I am proud of you Frieda. You have a cool head."

And then he was gone. She went in search of the reverend. Many people had seen him, but nobody could place him at that exact minute. She wandered about the deck, but there was no sign of him or her father. Should she return to Hans? She heard some people say they were coming up to the Gates of Hell, a place on the river where boats regularly went aground. The men said the captain knew what he was doing, he'd been sailing boats up and down the river for the last thirty years. Frieda didn't pay any attention, she figured if there was a fire onboard, it was more worrying than anything out in the water.

As she glanced toward the pilot house, she saw a boy trying to get the captain's attention. The boy was shouting, Frieda couldn't hear him over the music played by the band, but she could read his lips. He was shouting "fire" and pointing to the stairwell behind him. There she could see smoke but was it from a fire or the engines? She waited to see what the captain would do. If it were serious, he would leave the pilot house wouldn't he? A crewmember ran past her, pushing against her, but didn't apologize. She wouldn't have been able to describe what he looked like, he moved that fast. He seemed to be looking for someone as well.

Some people came up on deck complaining that smoke filled the room where beer was being served.

"How many lifeboats are on board?"

"Do you have life preservers for everyone?"

"I can't swim."

"What should we do?"

"Can't you stop the fire?"

Everyone spoke at once, but the crew didn't appear to hear any of them. Frieda wanted to ask questions too, but her father had told her to return to find Hans if people started to panic. She pushed her way through the crowd heading toward their seats, apologizing as she bumped into people. At times the swell of people carried her forward or to the side. Sometimes it was as if she couldn't feel the deck beneath her. She bit her lip and counted down from ten in an effort not to panic. As she moved, she realized the band had stopped playing. She didn't want to question why. She kept moving forward, refusing to look behind her. Maybe if she didn't see the fire, it wouldn't hurt them.

CHAPTER 65

*J*ust as Frieda reached where her brother had been sitting, a burst of flame exploded out of the steamer's lower port side. People screamed. Men, women and children. Frieda turned, frantically calling Hans' name. "Hans, come here. Where are you? *Papi*, are you there?"

But nobody answered. Frieda headed for the stairs, forgetting her father had told her to stay on the upper decks. But that was a disaster. She watched the captain take a couple of steps downward before he was forced by the heat and flames to retreat.

"Mother of God, please don't let *Papi* and Hans be down there," she prayed as she made her way back to their seats in the desperate hope her family had come back. There was a crowd gathering nearby as it was the farthest side from the flames, but no sign of her father or brother.

Then she spotted Reverend Haas. He seemed to be instructing people to move to the stern of the boat. She tried to push against the swarm of people now moving toward her. If she could speak to Rev Haas, he might know where her father and Hans were. She pushed, but the crowd was too much for her. Women clung to children with a death like grip. Frieda had to accept she wasn't going to get near to Reverend Haas. Not yet, anyway.

Terrified, Frieda stood near the stern, waiting and hoping her father and brother would find her. Women and children screamed around her. Some told of horrible experiences as they fought their way up from where the ice-cream room was. She heard the sounds of loud splashes. Moving closer to the rail, she saw people in the water. Why had they jumped? Then she looked over their heads to see what her eyes couldn't understand. A giant wall of flames. The people in the water had been left with little choice: jump or burn.

Frieda watched as panic broke out around her. People ran screaming to find children, others headed for life preservers. Some flung their children overboard and jumped in after them. She stood silent, watching and waiting, although she couldn't say why.

"Stay calm, stay calm," Reverend Haas shouted at his flock over and over again.

Frieda watched the man they all loved and respected move in the direction of the fire, against the way the crowd was moving. What was he doing?

"He's trying to close the doors of the main cabin. Maybe he thinks it will stop the fire?"

Frieda glanced at the man speaking. From what he wore, he looked like a member of the ship's crew.

"Can't you help him?

"Nah miss, he's wasting his time. We ain't got any way to beat a fire that big. Can you swim? That's your best bet now."

Frieda turned away in disgust. She saw some of the adults in the church trying to launch a lifeboat, but it seemed to be stuck. One of the men used a knife on some ropes but nothing seemed to work. She scanned the entire area again, not seeing her family in the faces of fear looking back at her.

Frieda glanced back at the water, there was a tugboat coming toward them. Would it be able to rescue anyone?

CHAPTER 66

*C*harlie drove to a point farther up the river where he knew of a nice café. They parked the car and sat watching the activities around them as they enjoyed three iced teas.

"This spot is perfect. They will be through hell's gate in a few minutes and we will be able to wave at our boy," Charlie said.

"Hell's gate?" Kathleen queried.

"It's a piece of water that can be difficult to navigate." Charlie seemed to realize what he was saying. "Only for those who aren't used to the river. The captain has been sailing the East River for over thirty years. He knows it like the back of his hand. No cause for alarm."

Kathleen glanced at Charlie's face, but he appeared to be genuinely unconcerned.

"See, there they are, coming through just fine." He

turned to his wife. "I know you are annoyed with Teddy, but it's nice to get outside and just sit for a while, isn't it? Without the children looking for attention or work worries."

"Yes, Charlie it is. Isn't it, Lily?"

Lily was staring at something in the distance. Kathleen poked her friend in the arm. But Lily ignored her and stood up.

"What's up with you? You won't be able to see Teddy from here."

"Charlie, why is there smoke coming out of that boat?" Lily pointed. "Charlie, that's the General Slocum. There's smoke belching out of it. Oh my God, please help our baby. It's on fire."

Charlie ran as close to the edge of the water as he could as Kathleen gripped Lily's arm. "They have to fuel the engines, darling. It could just be that."

"Kathleen, don't be an idiot," Lily retorted. "Look at the reactions of the tugboats. People are stopping and watching. Something is wrong. Teddy can't swim. The captain will have to get them on shore. Why isn't he making for shore?"

Kathleen didn't know what the captain was doing. It was impossible to see that far away, but she didn't dare voice that opinion. Lily was never unkind, but she was distraught. She looked around for Charlie but couldn't see him.

"Lily, let's get back to the car. Charlie is probably waiting for us there."

Lily couldn't move but remained frozen in place. Her cries had attracted the attention of some others. Kathleen saw a policeman. She hitched up her skirts and ran to him.

"Can you help us please. There seems to be trouble on the water. See?" Kathleen pointed in the direction of the boat. Black plumes of smoke were rising out of the stricken vessel leaving nobody in any doubt, there was a serious fire onboard.

"I will ring for help, missus. Don't go trying to be brave. Leave it to the professionals."

He was gone before Kathleen realized he thought she was going to try and swim. In this dress, she wouldn't get more than a few feet. She turned back to find her friends.

"Kathleen, one of the river men reckons the captain will try to get her to land, but finding a safe spot might be difficult. Please stay with Lily while I try to find out more," Charlie said.

"Of course. Good luck." Kathleen walked to find Lily, all the time praying for the ten-year-old boy she adored.

rieda climbed up on the rail, intending to use the height to try to pinpoint her family, but instead she was pushed over the side. She gripped the railing as tight as she could. If she let go, she would land in the water. Some mothers beside her were putting life preservers over their children's heads and then throwing them into the water. Frieda didn't see any of those thrown come back to the surface which is what should have happened when using life preservers. A female passenger passed her a life float.

"Put this on girl, it'll help you float."

Frieda shook her head. She didn't need one. She could swim. Should she jump? But what if *Papi* and Hans were looking for her?

"Have you seen my father? Or Hans?" she asked anyone she recognized but they shook their heads. She bit her lip, wondering what to do. People raced from one side of the steamer to the other to find their loved ones. Panic bread panic.

She looked down at the water. More people were jumping. Some by choice, some because the crowd pushed them in. Again, and again, she saw people landing on other swimmers, pushing the poor unfortunates into the water. If she was to have a chance, she had to jump far enough out to be able to swim alone. The ship didn't seem to be stopping, if anything it seemed to be moving faster. Why wasn't the captain heading for shore?

Frieda tore off her shoes, gave a last look around her, and taking a deep breath, jumped as far out as she could. The freezing water forced the air from her lungs, but she kept her mouth shut, holding her breath waiting to come back up to the surface.

As her head broke through, she saw she had landed well away from some of the bigger groups. She treaded water as she got her bearings. Then she started swimming toward a tug boat which seemed to be on their way to help.

"Help, please help," a woman screamed. Frieda turned in time to see the woman go under water, but she quickly resurfaced. "I can't swim. I've a baby."

Frieda couldn't let the woman die. She had to try and help her. Swimming carefully, she moved slowly toward the woman.

"Don't grab me, you'll pull both of us under," Frieda told her. "Give me the baby."

"No!" the woman said something else but as she was swallowing water, Frieda couldn't make out what she said. The woman went under again. Frieda tried to dive down to help her but there wasn't enough space. She broke through the water and, relieved, spotted the woman doing the same. Frieda held out her hand. "Try to float on your back, I will hold you, but you have to do what I say."

The woman nodded, terror making her eyes wide.

Frieda swam nearer the woman and anchoring her arm under the woman's chin, fought to carry them both toward the tug boat. The woman kicked and screamed, causing both of them to go under. Frieda let her go, only to try to go back and grab her again.

"Please trust me," she begged the woman. Whether the woman heard her or had fallen unconscious, she didn't know, but she pulled her toward the tug boat. As they got alongside it, some men helped pull the woman and child onboard. The woman still refused to release her baby.

"Come on girl, grab my hand."

Frieda shook her head. "I have to find my brother. Please help us. There were over a thousand people on the boat."

"A thousand?" the man looked to the Slocum which was like a blazing inferno by this stage.

"Yes. A lot of children. Please help them."

CHAPTER 68

*B*efore he could argue with her, Frieda turned and swam back toward the fiery boat. She encountered two small children, trying to swim but she could see the older child was tiring fast. He'd been using his strength to keep the younger one's face out of the water.

"Let me help. I'll take him, you swim to that boat. See it?"

The older boy nodded and reluctantly gave over his young charge to Frieda. She did the same as she had done with the woman, thanking her mother and father for making her learn to swim all those years ago.

Back and forth she went with another man from the tug boat. He was the only crew member who could swim. Together they got about ten people out of the water. On her last turn out, Frieda felt something grab her legs and pull her under the water, she kicked out, but the person held onto her. She was going to drown if she didn't get free. She kicked again with all her might and prayed hard. Suddenly, she felt the grip slacken and with an almighty shove she got free. By the time she broke the top of the water, she was breathing heavily.

"Girl you need to get back to the boat," the tug crew member said. "Let someone else help. Go on, love. God bless you."

Frieda knew she had to rest, if only for five minutes. She couldn't keep going. She spotted a young boy not too far from the boat so swam over to help pull him to safety. But when she got to him, she saw he was already gone, face down in the water. She still grabbed him and pulled him to the boat. He was someone's child and they would want to bury him.

CHAPTER 69

"Where is Teddy? Have you seen him? Has anyone seen my son?" Lily screamed as she ran from person to person along the shore line. There were bodies everywhere, mainly women and children. But no sign of Teddy.

"Lily you must go home. There is nothing you can do here. The firemen and police will do their jobs. We will wait at your house. It's the first place Teddy will come looking for you." Kathleen gripped Lily's arm and half pulled, half dragged her to a cab. She gave the cabbie Lily's address. Mini Mike was by her side just before she climbed in.

"We'll find them Miss Lily. You can count on us."

Lily glanced at her friend, but she couldn't say anything. Kathleen thanked Mike and closed the door of the cab. It took ages to get home with the streets blocked by those who had rushed to help as well as spectators.

"Charlie and the rest of the people looking will find them. Don't lose hope, Lily." But even as Kathleen spoke the words, she couldn't keep her voice from trembling. Granny Belbin had foreseen a great tragedy. What could be more tragic than a boat full of families enjoying a beautiful June day only to flounder with such horrendous loss of life? How many of those families would still be alive to see tomorrow? She squeezed her eyes shut, trying to keep the tears from falling.

But they didn't make it back to Lily's house.

"Kathleen, I can't go home. I have to be there. He might need me."

Before Kathleen could react, Lily instructed the cab driver to turn back.

"Kathleen, what if it was Patrick or any child in trouble? Wouldn't you have stayed?"

Kathleen nodded. "I will go back with you. I won't leave your side until we find Teddy, I promise."

Lily squeezed Kathleen's hand. Kathleen prayed hard Teddy would survive and they would find him soon.

They didn't see Mini Mike or Tommy when they returned but found a crowd gathered by the riverside.

"Where is he going? He'll drown. Someone stop him," a man shouted

But nobody paid any attention, their eyes on the boy who divested his clothes and shoes before diving into the water. They watched, each holding their breath, as the young boy swam out to a toddler. They cheered as the boy pulled the toddler to safety, bringing him back to shore. He handed the child over to a nurse before turning and heading back into the water. Again, and again he swam out and came back, sometimes with two children in his arms.

"Who is he?" someone asked.

"Hans Klunsberg. He's only ten. I didn't know he could swim. Oh no, it looks like someone is pulling him under." The man spoke with a German accent making Kathleen think he was from the same community as the heroic boy.

They watched, helpless as Hans fought someone in the water. It was a larger woman who appeared to be trying to use Hans as a life jacket but was precariously close to drowning both of them.

"Come on Hans, swim back to us please." A woman nearby shouted. Kathleen didn't know if she knew the boy or was just caught up in the momentum of what was happening.

Hans managed to loosen the woman's grip, but instead of swimming away from her, he put his arm around the woman and seemed to be trying to bring her to shore.

A woman screamed from the bank. "Someone help him. Please. He'll drown."

A policeman to one side of Lily stripped off his jacket and boots and ran into the water, closely followed by what looked like a nurse carrying a ladder. Kathleen immediately saw her intentions. She helped hold the ladder as they waded into the shallow waters. By using it as a bridge, they could attempt to reach some of those still stranded.

Kathleen lost sight of the young boy. She assumed the police officer must have ordered him out of the water and to safety.

CHAPTER 70

*K*athleen offered a hand to a girl who jumped off a tugboat nearing the shore.

"You should go to the hospital," Kathleen said. The young girl, who appeared to be about fourteen shook her head.

"I have to find Hans and *Papi*."

Before Kathleen could stop her, the girl made three more trips into the water before some hospital doctors insisted she rest.

A nurse put a blanket around the girl's shoulders. "We will sit on you to stop you going back in. You need to recover your strength. What's your name, little lady."

"Frieda."

Kathleen saw the girl try to argue but she was too

exhausted. She watched as a nurse gave Frieda something to drink, whiskey, judging by the reaction on the young girl's face.

Lily turned back to look at the water. Kathleen couldn't bear to watch the pain on her friend's face. Was her son one of those floating on the river or had someone like Frieda managed to save him?

"Lily, I think we should go home now. You're freezing. "

"Kathleen, I'd feel something wouldn't I? If he was dead? My heart would stop beating, wouldn't it?"

Kathleen handed her a mug of tea. "Someone sent this down to the workers. I don't think they will miss one cup. Drink it, Lily. You won't be any good to anyone if you get ill."

Lily didn't argue. She didn't have the strength for anything.

"They just took that girl who saved so many people up to the hospital. She'll be fine but they think she swallowed a lot of water. She was wonderful, wasn't she?"

Lily didn't seem to hear what Kathleen was saying. All day and into the night, they stayed by the riverside, helping where they could. Kathleen tried to get Lily to go into the hospital fearing her friend was in severe shock but Lily refused.

"I can't leave, Kathleen. I sense Teddy is nearby. If I go, I might..."Lily stared at the water, "I might never see him again."

Kathleen knew Lily wasn't being logical but she could see her friend was convinced she had to stay. Kathleen got a blanket and hot drink from one of the volunteers and insisted Lily sit down.

Together they held hands. The police officers told them they had stopped bringing out survivors hours earlier. Now they were clearing the water of bodies. Kathleen watched as they wrote identifications on the labels before attaching them to the bodies. Someone said it was to give the authorities a chance to identify the poor unfortunates.

"Richard called me," Inspector Griffin announced as he came upon Lily and Kathleen.

"Where is Richard? Have you heard anything from Charlie?" Lily asked.

"Charlie is doing the rounds of local hospitals and police stations. Anywhere they took the survivors. I'm sorry, Lily but there is no news yet." Inspector Griffin couldn't hold her gaze. He looked to Kathleen.

Kathleen took a breath. "Richard is in surgery isn't he?"

"Yes he is. He is working on the worst of the burn victims. Those that can't yet be moved. Some are on their way to Bellevue and other hospitals. This one isn't designed to cope with fires."

Lily stared past them at the river. Kathleen followed her gaze. Was Teddy out there somewhere?

"Lily, I think it's time you went home. The other children are bound to be scared and will want their mother. There is no point in staying here." Kathleen spoke softly, but still she saw Lily clench her fists.

"Teddy needs me more."

"Lily, he may be on his way home." Kathleen looked to Inspector Griffin for help.

"Come on Miss Lily," Inspector Griffin said. "I'll take you home and then do a tour of the stations. Maybe someone picked him up."

Kathleen thought Lily would argue but instead her friend's shoulders slumped. Lily had given up and that knowledge scared Kathleen almost more than the sights she had seen this night.

Lily's knees buckled, so Inspector Griffin had to pick her up and carry her like a child. The cab took no time to get home, possibly due to the presence of the police inspector. Soon they were standing on the sidewalk outside Lily's home.

"Kathleen, how can I face my children? Laurie especially. He will be devastated I came back without Teddy."

Before Kathleen could speak, they heard Laurie shouting.

"Mom, thank God you're home." Laurie came running out the door. "Dad isn't here, and the girls were crying. Cook tried to stop them but they kept asking for you. Where's Teddy? Did you find him?"

Lily couldn't speak. She shook her head. Laurie flung himself into her arms.

"You will, Mom. You'll find him."

They walked arm in arm into the house, Kathleen and Inspector Griffin following behind.

CHAPTER 71

*K*athleen and Lily put the other children to bed with a promise to wake them up as soon as there was any news. Kathleen's heart broke for them all, but especially Laurie. He kept telling Lily that Teddy was still alive.

"He's my twin. I'd know if he was dead. He's scared and his hands hurt. But he's alive."

The adults didn't pay much attention to Laurie. Lily seemed numb. She didn't cry or talk. She sat, white-faced, staring at the window. Charlie was still searching the hospitals and the morgue. The continuous stream of visitors brought reports of complete chaos in the hospitals and morgues as the city dealt with the greatest tragedy it had known. Over one thousand dead. Many of those saved had suffered horrible burns and some were half-drowned.

"Father Nelson, I have to go to the hospital and see

Richard and Patrick. I won't be long. Will you stay with Lily?"

"Of course, Kathleen. Take your time. You should rest too. You've been awake for hours."

"I can rest when we know. My heart breaks for Lily. I feel I should stay but I need to see my family."

"Go. You can come back later, and I will stay with her in the meantime."

athleen took a cab to the hospital where Richard worked. Patrick had volunteered to help at the hospital as soon as the news hit. When she arrived, Richard was in surgery, but she got to hug Patrick. He was white with shock and tiredness, but he refused to come home.

"Sorry Mom, but there is too much to be done here. It's not just the victims, but some of the families of those missing are in shock. They need to be looked after."

"What can I do?" Kathleen asked, not commenting on the fact Patrick had called her "Mom". It showed just how upset he was.

Patrick glanced at her as if he wanted to say something but was afraid to. "Is there any news of Teddy? Dad told me he was missing."

"No darling. None yet."

"Mom, there are lots of children here. Do you think you should ask them if they saw Teddy? Some might know?'

"Did you see his friend Kevin?" Even as she asked, she knew it was a stupid question. Patrick didn't know Teddy's school friends.

"I'll take you to them, shall I?"

"Yes, please but then I will have to get back to Lily. She is in a bad way."

Patrick escorted her down to where some children who didn't seem injured were waiting. They were very quiet, which in itself was worrying. Given what had happened, they should have been crying or screaming.

Kathleen moved among them, asking them if they needed anything. Some didn't answer her, others asked if she had seen their parents. A couple didn't speak good English and she wasn't able to make herself understood. Then she found a girl she recognized.

"You are the young swimmer. I saw you rescue some people. I'm Kathleen Green."

"Frieda Klunsberg."

"Are you alright? Can I get you anything?" Kathleen glanced at the girl's bandaged hands. "Are you in pain? Maybe I could find a nurse."

"I can't find my father or brother. Have you seen them? Someone said Hans helped to save some people. He is a good swimmer too."

"Is he about ten years old?"

Hope flared in Frieda's eyes. "Yes, he is. About this tall and has sandy colored hair. Did you see him?"

"I saw him rescue some children. And a lady. But that was hours ago. He didn't seem to be injured. Could he have gone home looking for you and your father?"

Frieda stood up. "I didn't think of that. I will go and find out. Thank you, Mrs. Green."

"Wait. You can't go alone. Where do you live?"

"Klein—I mean, Little Germany."

"I can take you. I will go with you in the cab."

"Aren't your looking for someone?" Frieda asked.

"My husband and son both work here. I just needed to see them. A friend's child is missing. Teddy, Theodore Doherty. You don't know him, do you?"

Frieda shook her head.

"He's ten like your brother. He shouldn't have been at the picnic. His parents told him not to go but... well boys will be boys."

Kathleen asked the nurse if it was alright to take Frieda home. She explained the girl was looking for her family.

"She is physically fine but don't leave her alone. There are many who won't be returning to Little Germany ever again."

Kathleen swallowed hard before returning to find Frieda. She plastered a smile on her face. "Right, let's get you home. Did you hurt your legs?"

"No, but I lost my shoes." Frieda grimaced as she stepped on something.

Kathleen glanced at the floor before almost walking into Inspector Griffin.

"Kathleen, what are you doing here? Did you find him?"

"No Inspector, not yet. Richard is working. I came down to see him. This young lady is Frieda Klunsberg. She was one of the heroines today. I saw her save many people."

"Well done, miss. Where are you going now?"

"We are going back to Little Germany. Frieda is looking for her father and brother, Hans. He saved some people too. Your father will be very proud of both of you."

Inspector Griffin looked at Frieda, respect shining from his eyes.

"Miss Kathleen, hold on. Let me get two of my guys to take you."

"There is no danger, is there?" Kathleen asked.

"No, but there are large crowds of people on the streets. Alone you will have trouble getting to Frieda's home."

"Thank you, Inspector. You always turn up just where you are needed."

Her compliment pleased him, judging by the expression in his eyes.

CHAPTER 73

*I*nspector Griffin hadn't been joking. They were met by crowds upon crowds of people, all searching for someone. Frieda shrank back a little, not from the crowds Kathleen guessed, but the reality there were so many missing.

"It's this block here. Thank you so much."

"I will go up with you. I don't want to leave you alone." Kathleen didn't add "just in case there is nobody home".

They walked up the stairs, Frieda apologizing as they walked.

"Frieda, I grew up not far from here. Please don't worry. Is this it?"

Frieda stood outside a closed door. The girl seemed to lose all her bravery.

"Yes," she whispered.

"Would you like me to open the door?"

Frieda nodded.

Kathleen knocked but there was no reply. She turned the handle and the door opened. It wasn't locked. Was that a good sign?

"Frieda. There you are. Oh, my goodness I was so worried about you." The woman came flying at Frieda, almost knocking Kathleen off her feet.

"I'm fine, Mrs. Sauer but I hurt my hands."

Kathleen winced as the woman had grabbed the child's arms. Mrs. Sauer appeared to be a neighbor.

"Oh Frieda. I'd lost hope when we didn't hear anything. Nobody seemed to have seen you. Not that many have come back."

"Are father and Hans not here?" Frieda asked. The girl looked around as if expecting her family to jump out and say surprise.

"No, *Liebling*. Nobody came home." Mrs. Sauer didn't look at Frieda but glanced away.

Kathleen coughed to get rid of the lump in her throat.

"Mrs. Sauer. I found Frieda in the hospital. She was very brave, she saved a number of people from the river. So did her brother. I believe I saw him in action, although I don't know for sure. We've never met. My name is Kathleen Green. I work at the sanctuary."

"With Father Nelson?"

"I know Father Nelson, yes."

"Thank you, Mrs. Green, for bringing Frieda home. I will take care of her now."

Kathleen felt she was being dismissed, but the woman wasn't being rude just fretful. She turned to Frieda, "Please do come see us at the sanctuary if you ever need anything. Thank you for what you did today. I hope you find your father and brother soon."

Kathleen walked out the door and down the stairs. The neighbor came running after her.

"Mrs. Green, please wait."

"Yes?" Kathleen turned to look at the woman, horrified to find tears streaming down her face.

"I didn't mean to be rude up there. I just, well we were told they have found Frieda's father. He won't be coming back today or any other. I haven't heard anything about Hans. What will I say to her? If Hans doesn't come back, she will be left alone with Lottie and that child will be in Heaven soon."

"I am so sorry. Please, if there is anything I can do, come and find me. I have to get back to my friend's house now. Her little boy is also missing."

Mrs. Sauer crossed herself. "So many gone. Nobody could have guessed when they left here yesterday. All of them so happy. And now...I pray you find your boy."

The woman was gone before Kathleen could correct her. Thankfully Inspector Griffin's two men had waited and were able to secure her a cab. Everywhere people waited on street corners, hoping for news. She couldn't bear it. She pushed herself as far as she could into the seat, hoping and willing Teddy would be found alive.

CHAPTER 74

The cab turned the corner onto Lily's street. Kathleen sat forward, taking out her purse to pay the driver. She spotted someone on the street, dragging his heels, it was a child.

"Stop."

The cab stopped but almost before he did, Kathleen was out the door.

"Teddy! Oh my goodness, you're alive. Thank God. Let me look at you. You've hurt your hands."

Teddy glanced at his hands. "I had to hold on to the boat's rail or I would have gone into the water, it was hot." He swallowed before looking at Kathleen, "Aunty Kathleen, are my parents going to kill me?"

"No, my darling boy, they are going to be thrilled beyond belief. Come on, let's get you home. Why are you on your own?"

"I couldn't find anyone."

Those words chilled her to the bone. She took his hand gently in hers and pulled him into the cab with instructions to the driver to hurry to Lily's house.

"Lily, Charlie, everyone. Look who I found." Kathleen knew she was screaming like a fishwife, but she didn't care. The cabbie got down and ran toward the house. Kathleen helped Teddy from the cab, but no sooner had he set his feet on the sidewalk when he was whisked into his father's arms.

"Teddy, oh my goodness. You're alive."

"Teddy, darling. Oh, thank God." Lily grabbed for her son's hands. Kathleen quickly intervened.

"He's hurt Lily, watch his hands. You should take him to the hospital, so they don't get infected."

The cabbie was ordered to do just that and before anyone had time to think, Charlie and Lily were rushing off in the cab back to Richard at the hospital. He was the only doctor they would trust with Teddy.

Kathleen hugged herself tight and then got a hug from Father Nelson.

"Tis a wonderful thing you did, Kathleen Green. Finding that boy."

"I didn't find him, Father, he was almost home. And he was exactly as Laurie described, scared and his hands were hurting."

"That's twins for you. Shall we go in and tell the children?"

Kathleen let the old man lead her into the house. The children were asleep, so they decided not to wake them. They sat in the living room waiting for the others to come home. Cook made them tea and sandwiches and to her surprise, Kathleen found she was ravenous.

"Thank you, Cook."

"I'd always do anything for you, Miss Kathleen, but now you are my hero."

Her words reminded her of Frieda. What was she going to do now?

"Speaking of heroes, that reminds me, Father. I was in Little Germany before I found Teddy. It is so sad, there are people everywhere on the streets looking for their friends and family. I think your friend Reverend Haas could do with some help."

"Did he survive?"

"Oh." Kathleen didn't know. She'd just assumed he had, but why would he when so many died? "I guess I should have said his congregation need the help."

"I will go down there first thing in the morning," Father Nelson said. "I think everyone will forgive me for waiting for our friends to come home."

Kathleen didn't want to be alone, so she was grateful the old priest saw it that way.

he next morning, Lily hadn't returned, so Kathleen made her way to the hospital, leaving Cook in charge of the children. When she arrived, she bumped into Frieda.

"Frieda, how are you? Did you find your brother?"

Frieda said nothing, just stared at her. Kathleen looked around and recognized Mrs. Sauer. The woman was weeping openly.

"So many of our friends never came home. Frieda came down here as someone said Hans was here. He was but...he was too badly injured. He died about an hour ago."

"Oh, the poor child. I thought I saw him rescuing people in the water. I must have mistaken him for someone else." Kathleen felt awful as she had given Frieda false hope.

"No, you did see him. They believe he rescued at

least five people, maybe more. But he jumped in again to save a baby and got hit by something. They think it might have been a tugboat. They didn't realize something hurt him bad until he collapsed. The poor boy. He was a hero."

"Oh Mrs. Sauer, I am so sorry. Can I do anything to help Frieda?"

"No, I will look after her for the moment. You could pray for the baby. Her name is Elsa. She is the only member of her family to live. Her mother, father, grandmother, sisters, brothers. All gone. All gone." The woman couldn't restrain the tears any longer and sobbed into her hands. Kathleen didn't know what to do.

Frieda took Mrs. Sauer's arm. "I will take her home to her husband."

Frieda's lack of emotion scared Kathleen. She was torn between going after the girl and staying at the hospital.

"Please help Elsa. Don't let Hans die in vain," Frieda said.

Kathleen promised she wouldn't leave the baby.

At first, she couldn't find baby Elsa, but Patrick came to her rescue.

"Poor thing is only about six months old. She has some burns, but they don't seem to be too bad. She would have drowned but for some kid. He jumped in and saved her. Imagine that."

"That kid was the ten-year-old brother of a girl I met last night. He died."

"Ten?" Patrick said. "The same age as Teddy."

The thought silenced both of them. Patrick took Kathleen to where baby Elsa was resting. Kathleen couldn't believe how tiny the child was in the cot. She put her hand out to touch her and Elsa grabbed at her fingers and wouldn't let go. The strength of her touch was amazing.

"Little fighter, she is, Mrs. Green. I wish some of our older patients were as brave." The nurse smiled as she spoke, telling Kathleen she wasn't being serious.

"Can I stay with her? Richard is in surgery, Patrick is working and I have nowhere else to be."

"To be honest, we need as much help as we can get," the nurse said. "We are overrun, not just with patients from the tragedy itself, but family members looking for their lost ones. We aren't about to turn down help."

Kathleen stayed by Elsa's side, changing her diaper and feeding her as required. When the baby started to cry, Kathleen picked her up and cuddled her close. She waited for someone to come and ask about Elsa, but nobody did.

CHAPTER 76

*W*hen Richard arrived on the ward some time later, he found Kathleen and the baby fast asleep.

"Darling, go home and rest. You have been here for hours."

"Elsa needs me. She has no one else."

"She has the nurses and doctors to care for her. Come on, let's get you home. You can come back tomorrow," Richard said.

Kathleen shook her head. "I can't leave her, Richard. I promised I would make sure Hans didn't die in vain."

"Who is Hans?"

"Frieda's brother. I will explain later. For now, I need to stay here. Can you check Elsa for me please? Is she in pain?"

"Darling, there is a team of doctors and nurses looking after her."

"Yes, but you are the best. Can you just have a look, please?"

Richard picked Elsa up, and she snuggled into his neck. The look of shock on his face was quickly followed by an expression that almost made Kathleen cry. She watched as her husband tenderly examined the baby.

"She seems like a fighter. The burns are superficial, thank goodness. I don't like her cough, but hopefully she will recover soon. She is a pretty little thing, isn't she?"

"She's gorgeous." Kathleen looked around to make sure nobody was listening. "Richard, this isn't the right time, but there never is a good time. Elsa is alone. Her parents and family died in the fire. Do you think they might let us adopt her?"

Richard looked shocked, then concerned.

"Kathleen darling, she could have extended family who want to take her. You are tired, we all are. It's been a horrendous day and night. I know you already love this baby, but it's far too soon to be thinking that way."

Kathleen stroked Elsa's cheek.

"I know I shouldn't be, and I feel guilty for even mentioning it, but when the people from her community come around, can I please offer to bring her home and look after her?"

Concern written all over his face, her husband

traced his finger up and down her arm. She touched his face with her hand.

"I know you are worried I will get my heart broken again," she said. "That's a risk I will take. I can't help feeling I was supposed to meet Frieda and now Elsa. I think things are connected. Don't laugh. I know it sounds silly. I also hate the fact so many people died, but maybe this is God's plan. For us to have our baby. I mean, I don't think he killed all those people but..." She wasn't about to admit, maybe this was the tragedy Granny had predicted. Granny had said the young girl would be involved with a fire. She had assumed Granny was talking about Mia but maybe she had been talking about Elsa. But then Granny had told her to be careful what she wished for. Had she caused this accident by wishing for a baby. She didn't want to think it might be her fault. Maybe messing with reading the future had caused this catastrophe. But no, that was silly. Nobody knew what would happen. Accidents, even those as horrible as this one, happened.

"I understand what you are saying, but let's take our time, Kathleen. You of all people know this whole process will take some time to work out. The authorities and the church are likely to be involved. It is far too early to speculate now."

Richard replaced the blanket Elsa has just kicked off. Kathleen watched him, thinking what a wonderful father he would be.

"I know all that in my head. But in my heart, I just want to love her and protect her."

"Do that darling, but also protect yourself. I couldn't bear you to suffer another heartbreak."

She knew he was referring to Mia. He'd held her so tenderly when she'd cried, explaining how it felt to give Mia to Shane. How guilty she was at the thought of being jealous of her brother and knowing Mia was getting the best family ever.

CHAPTER 77

athleen stayed in the hospital another few hours before giving into pressure from Richard and the nurses on the ward to go home and get some sleep. She didn't sleep, but she had a bath and changed her clothes. She also went to the store and bought some new clothes for Elsa and a cuddly toy rabbit for her cot. When she came back, she was relieved to find the baby was doing well.

"Her lungs seem to be clearing a little," one of the nurses told her. "They don't sound as congested."

Kathleen stayed with the child for a little while before going to find Lily. Teddy was in the children's ward, his hands all bandaged up. He looked so tiny and pale in the bed. Lily was sitting beside him, her hand on his leg as if she could prevent him leaving her.

"Lily?" Kathleen whispered.

Lily raised a tear-stained face, taking a minute to recognize Kathleen.

"We were so lucky Kathleen. Kevin and his family haven't been found. I don't know how Teddy got off that boat. He says a girl helped him out of the water. She could swim."

Kathleen glanced at Teddy before turning her attention back to Lily.

"I wonder was it Frieda?"

"Who?" Lily asked.

"The girl I took home the other night. She was here yesterday. Looking for her brother. He was too badly injured to survive. Her father died too."

"Where is she now? Can I talk to her? Maybe give her a reward?" Lily asked, looking around as if Frieda might show up.

"I was going to call to her home to check on her. I will ask her if she will come to see Teddy."

"Thank you, Kathleen. I don't want to leave his side. I know he's out of danger, but still. I have to be here. It's all so horrible."

CHAPTER 78

*K*athleen took a cab to Little Germany, but because of the sheer number of people around, she had to get out and walk. She saw newspaper reporters hassling people to find out every little detail. Some men looked shell shocked as they wandered from person to person, asking for news of their families. More than once, she heard a man cry out as his neighbor told him the news he'd been dreading. Picking up her skirts, she hurried to Frieda's address. When she knocked on the door, she was relieved the girl opened it. Her face fell when she saw Kathleen.

"I thought you might have been *Papi,* even though I know he's dead. I saw Hans' body, but not *Papi.* It is like it isn't real. You know?"

Kathleen nodded. She handed the girl the food she had brought with her. A small basket seemed such a pitiful response to the loss of a father and brother. Frieda took the basket and put it on the table. "I will bring it to Mrs. Sauer. She makes me eat with her family." Then she looked at Kathleen. "Why did you come? Is it Elsa? Did she die too?"

"No, she didn't. She is doing well, although still in hospital. I came because I think you may have rescued my friend's son. She would love to meet you, but doesn't want to leave the hospital. Could you come?"

When Frieda hesitated, Kathleen continued.

"You would help a lot. Some children and adults in the hospital don't speak great English. Maybe you could help the nurses by translating what they need to be told. It's scary being in hospital, but when you don't know what the people are saying..."

Frieda seemed numb. Kathleen wondered if the girl should be in hospital. It was better than her being in this room all by herself, waiting and waiting for someone who wasn't coming home.

"If you came with me, I will stay with you. You won't be alone and if you want to come home at any time, I will take you."

"Why?"

"Frieda, you helped people without asking why. It's something we just do. Isn't it?"

Frieda nodded. "I better tell Mrs. Sauer where I am going. She is very upset. She was so fond of Hans and Lottie."

"Lottie?"

"My little sister. She's sick. They think she has consumption. *Papi* put her in hospital a week ago to see if they could make her better."

Kathleen couldn't believe the fourteen-year-old had so much hardship, yet hadn't broken down. She figured the storm would come and swore to be with Frieda when it did.

"I will go with you to see Mrs. Sauer. She may know of other ways the sanctuary can help." Kathleen outlined what the sanctuary was and what it did over a cup of coffee at Mrs. Sauer's house. She found out Father Nelson had been to the church and taken the service as Reverend Haas was ill. The reverend had lost his wife and sister in the fire and many members of his congregation.

"Poor Mary also died." Mrs. Sauer wrung her hands together. She looked at Kathleen. "Mary Abendschein, she was the one who organized everything. It may have been a blessing in her case. I don't think that sweet lady could have lived with the fact she organized the picnic that killed so many."

"It wasn't her fault. It was the ship and those crew members," Frieda said. "*Papi* said they didn't handle the fire correctly. It was one of the last things he said to Hans. They should have kept the door closed."

Kathleen didn't know what Frieda was talking about, but it seemed like the girl should speak to one of the investigators who was looking into the cause of the fire. "Charlie, my friend Lily's husband, works for a legal firm. He will know people who will want to speak to you about the trip, Frieda. For now, let's get back to the hospital. Mrs. Sauer, if you could get a few of the ladies from your community to make a list of things you need or who we can help, please come to the sanctuary."

"I will Mrs. Green, and thank you for looking after my community."

"It's our community Mrs. Sauer. We are all New Yorkers."

Mrs. Sauer cried once more so Kathleen bundled Frieda out the door. It was time for a change of scenery.

CHAPTER 79

$\mathcal{A}$s they made their way back to the hospital, Frieda told Kathleen of her hopes to become a doctor and then a nurse and how her father had been against them.

"I would give it all up if I could see him again. I loved him so."

"He loved you too, I'm sure. He would be so proud of you and your bother for saving so many people, Frieda. I think becoming a doctor would be wonderful."

"Yes, but now it will never happen. I have nobody left."

Kathleen held the girl's hand tight but didn't say a word. Now wasn't the time to make promises.

When they reached the ward, Teddy was sitting up in bed, both Charlie and Lily by his bedside.

"Teddy, I am so glad to see you awake. How are your hands?"

"Fine, thank you Aunty Kathleen. Oh, you're the girl who saved me, I remember your hair."

Frieda stepped forward. "I am glad you lived. You have strong legs. I still have a bruise where you kicked me."

Teddy turned scarlet as the adults smiled.

"I apologize. I thought you were trying to grab onto me. So many people in the water..." his words trailed off as his eyes filled with tears. Before anyone could react, Frieda flung herself at him and gathered him close careful not to hurt his hands.

"You must forget what you saw. It's over now. You don't have to be scared now. You will be fine. It is okay." Over and over the girl mumbled words of comfort to Teddy until his sobs subsided. Then she wiped the tears from her own face.

"I had a little brother just your age."

Charlie coughed as Lily and Kathleen blew their noses.

"Miss, we owe you a huge debt," Charlie said putting his arm around Lily. "Without your bravery, we could have lost our son. I don't know how to repay you."

"I don't want money." Frieda stood up.

"I didn't mean to offend you." Charlie turned red and looked to Kathleen.

"Frieda, Charlie was just trying to say thank you. He is the man I wanted you to speak to." Kathleen turned to Charlie. "Frieda's brother was one of the first to spot the fire. He told his father about it. Frieda says her father said the crew did the wrong thing. I thought you would know who should hear her story."

Charlie turned his attention to Frieda. "There will be an investigation and they will need to hear your testimony, but for now, keep this to yourself. I wouldn't want the wrong people to hear."

Kathleen saw the terror in the girl's eyes. She could have slapped Charlie, but he was too caught up in everything that was happening to think clearly. Lily obviously thought the same as she hissed, "Charlie!"

Then Lily turned to Frieda, "For now, Frieda, please come and stay with my husband and myself. I won't take no for an answer. Kathleen told us about your father and brother. I am so sorry. For the next few days, it will be very busy at the sanctuary and around Little Germany. People are going to be asking a lot of questions. You won't have time to rest. Please stay in our home as our guest."

Frieda shook her head, but Teddy spoke up, grabbing her by the hand despite the pain it caused him.

"Please say yes. I would like someone there who knows how horrible it was. I can't talk to my twin or my younger sisters. Please."

It was obvious Frieda couldn't bear to say no to Teddy.

"Okay, I will come and stay with you for a few nights. But then I must help my community. They need help. So many didn't come home."

"We will all help," Kathleen insisted. "Lily, I spoke with one of Frieda's neighbors. She will put a list together of what the families need. Also, I have told her about the sanctuary. We will have to be prepared for several children to come and stay for a while. Their parents may have to stay in hospital, those who still have a family. The rest will have to be adopted."

Lily nodded.

"Frieda, would you like to come and see Elsa?" Kathleen asked before explaining to the others. "Frieda's brother Hans died saving a baby. Her name is Elsa. Her parents didn't survive. She is on a ward upstairs."

"Oh, the poor baby. Frieda, go with Kathleen if you would like to. We will be here until the nurse tells us to leave. Then I will introduce you to Teddy's family. They are dying to meet his hero."

Frieda's cheeks turned red before she walked away. Kathleen gave Teddy one last smile before following Frieda up to see baby Elsa. She kept her fingers crossed that Charlie and Lily could help Frieda through the rough days ahead.

CHAPTER 80

Two weeks had passed since the day Lily had almost lost her son. She was still really angry and the newspapers weren't helping.

"I still can't believe anyone could be so negligent. The fire hoses fell apart, the lifeboats were wired to the davits. It's a wonder more weren't killed."

Lily glanced at her husband, her heart beating faster. They'd come so close to losing their son. How lucky they were compared to so many other families.

"What do you think will happen, Charlie?"

"The captain will go to jail, but the real villains will get away with it. Same as always. The inspection certificates were signed on behalf of the two inspectors not by them. Whoever signed won't be held accountable. Nor will the steamboat owners, although they should have replaced all the life vests and other safety features."

Lily wanted to scream over the unfairness of it all. "I can't believe the life jackets didn't work."

"Lily, not only did they not work, but they lead to the death of many of the victims. When cork is wet, it floats. But when cork turns to dust, like it was in those life jackets, when it gets wet it acts just like dirt. It gets heavier. Putting on the life jackets only hastened their deaths."

"Oh, my goodness. I can't believe anyone would let people onto a boat that wasn't safe."

"Believe it. It happens all the time, but until rich or famous people are killed, nothing will change. Anyway, let's not talk about it anymore. How was your day at the sanctuary?"

"Sad. There are quite a few German children joining the next orphan train. Some of those who survived the disaster were left alone. No parents or grandparents to take them in. They have nowhere else to go. Father Nelson was in contact with some people in Yorkville and other German communities and is placing as many of the children as he can in those areas. At least they will grow up with their language and culture, but some will have to go on the train."

"It is just horrible to lose your family and then your home. Those poor kids. I wish we could take some of them into our home."

Lily rose to kiss her husband on the head, "I know you do. I feel the same, but we have enough with the twins and the girls. I wonder how Kathleen and Richard are faring?"

Charlie pulled her down onto his lap. "Stop fretting, Lily. What is meant to be, will be."

CHAPTER 81

Kathleen couldn't believe her ears as she sat in front of the Judge. He'd said yes.

"Richard, is it true? Elsa is ours?" she whispered to her husband.

"Yes, darling. We can bring her home tomorrow. Are you happy?"

Happy? That was an understatement. She couldn't believe they were going to let her keep her baby. Elsa was hers from the minute she had held her hand the day after the tragedy.

Richard took her hand and led her from the Judges chambers.

"You're shivering. Are you coming down with a fever?" he asked.

"No, just excited. And feeling a little guilty. I can't help thinking I played a part in the General Slocum tragedy."

Richard spun her around to face him. "Kathleen Green, never say that again. You are not to blame for what happened. Those that failed to inspect the boat, or make sure the life preservers were up to date, they are to blame. You are as innocent as Elsa."

"But Granny Belbin..."

"Is an eccentric old lady. Put it out of your mind and let's celebrate our good fortune. Shall we go out to dinner or would you like to pick up Patrick and go and see Lily?"

Kathleen hugged her husband. He knew her so well. She had to share the news with her best friend. Patrick was at the hospital. There were still many patients fighting for their lives after the disaster and the nursing staff needed all the help they could get. Patrick said Frieda was a huge asset as she was able to act as translator. The two of them often worked together and had developed a good friendship.

Soon they were standing outside Lily's house. Patrick knocked at the door.

As soon as Lily opened the door, Kathleen apologized for turning up. "Sorry it's so late but we had to share our news."

Lily opened the door wider to let them all file into the sitting room. Charlie rose to greet them.

"Is everything all right?"

"Yes, Charlie, more than all right. Oh, Lily you will never guess. They said yes. We can adopt baby Elsa. She can come home with us."

Lily gathered Kathleen in her arms, hugging her as the tears streamed down both their faces.

"All her family died on the boat. Reverend Haas could confirm she lost her parents, her aunt and uncle and even her grandmother. It is so tragic."

"It is Kathleen, but she couldn't have found a better mother. Or father." Lily glanced at Richard. "But where is she?"

"Still in the hospital. Just a precaution as we don't know how her little lungs were affected. She seems fine, but they want to be sure and then the paperwork has to be completed. We can bring her home with us tomorrow. I can't wait. At last we will have our baby." Kathleen put her arm around Patrick. "Our son will have a new sister."

"He might even help change her diapers," Lily teased as Patrick's face turned bright red.

"No, thanks Mrs. Doherty. I will leave that to Mom. Are the twins still up?"

"Yes, they are. Teddy was feeling rather sore today."

Richard glanced at her, concern written all over his face. Kathleen squeezed his hand.

"He will be fine, Richard, thanks to you and your team." Lily hugged Richard. "The blisters are healing. I think he will have scars but compared to what could have happened he was lucky."

"Frieda said she came around to visit with him a few times. Her and Patrick have become quite friendly.

She helps at the hospital." Kathleen spoke as she sat down.

"Frieda is wonderful. She has accepted Charlie's donation toward her school fees and will train as a doctor when she is a little older. We asked her to come and live with us, but she declined. She accepted a room in the sanctuary."

"That's wonderful, Lily." Kathleen glanced at Richard, "Patrick didn't tell us that."

"I think she wants to keep it quiet for now. There are still so many funerals going on. When she is finished at the hospital, she will work at the sanctuary, helping the children get ready for the orphan train. She said she wants to do it until she can start back at school in September. I thought it might be too much, given how she lost her own siblings, but she says it helps. She is a very strong young woman."

Charlie moved and put his arm around his wife. "She reminds me of someone we all know and love."

"Charlie! I am not like her. Frieda is stubborn."

Lily's cheeks turned red as they all laughed. Kathleen suggested Richard and Charlie retire to Charlie's study.

"I think our wives want to speak in private, old man," Charlie said as he escorted Richard out of the room. "Let's have a drink. It's an Irish tradition, they say we must wet your new baby's head."

Silence lingered between the women until Lily

spoke up. "What's wrong, Kathleen. You aren't having second thoughts, are you?"

"About Elsa, no of course not. I just wanted to ask you something and didn't want the men to hear me. They will think I am being silly."

"You silly? I doubt it." Lily fell silent.

Kathleen wetted her suddenly dry mouth. "Lily, do you think Granny did see into the future? I mean she saw Pieter and Mia and she said I would get a baby following a tragedy." Kathleen's voice shook. It was one thing Richard telling her none of this was her fault but what if she had started something when she asked Granny to read the leaves.

Lily laughed but smothered it quickly as Kathleen looked at her.

"Sorry Kathleen, but that is the dumbest thing you have ever asked me. If Granny could really read the future, do you think she would still be living in Hell's Kitchen? Not likely. She would be living in some palace somewhere reading the leaves of the rich and famous. It's just a whole load of superstitious nonsense. Nothing more."

Kathleen sighed. She wondered if Lily was right. The sensible side of her brain believed she was but somewhere inside she wondered.

"Come on. Stop thinking about four leaved clovers and little green men and let's go find our husbands. We should celebrate your good news. After tomorrow, having a baby around all the time will make you too tired to want to party."

Kathleen accepted Lily's arm and together they went to find their families and celebrate their happiness.

EPILOGUE

SEPTEMBER 1904

Kathleen Green shifted baby Elsa in her arms. Her adopted daughter was growing heavier as the months passed by.

"Miss Kathleen, want me to carry her?"

Kathleen smiled at Mini Mike, he doted on her daughter just as did on all children. "No thanks, Mike. I can manage, if you can knock on the door. Do it loudly, as Granny's hearing isn't as good as it was."

Just as she said the words, the door opened.

"Nothing wrong with my hearing, Kathleen Collins. I heard every word you said." Granny stood on the doorstep, hands on her hips, a scowl on her face. "Are you going to let her talk about me like that, Michael?"

Mike grinned at Kathleen before giving Granny a hug. "I got to go and speak to a fella about a job. I will

be back in an hour to collect you Miss Kathleen.
Granny, put a smile on your face. You'll scare Elsa."

Kathleen didn't get a chance to tell Mike she
wouldn't be here for an hour. He had already disappeared into one of the side streets.

"Who?" Granny asked, peering at the bundle in
Kathleen's arms.

"My daughter, Elsa."

Granny turned pale but quickly regained her color.
Kathleen wondered had she imagined it. Granny held
the door as Kathleen entered the room. Only when
Granny had closed the door behind them, did she
speak.

"The baby I saw in the leaves. Let me hold her."
Granny's tone suggested it was an order not a request.

"Sit down first. She's heavier than she looks." Kathleen held Elsa tight until Granny did as she was bid.

"It's not like I never held a baby before. I ain't going
to drop her." Granny muttered as she made herself
comfortable on the stuffed chair before holding out her
arms.

Kathleen placed the sleeping child into the
outstretched arms. All at once, Elsa opened her eyes.
Kathleen held her breath expecting the baby to squeal
in protest but silence reined.

Elsa's eyes locked with Granny's making Kathleen
feel as if she was intruding on a special moment.
Granny muttered something, it didn't sound like
English. Kathleen folded her arms in an attempt to stop

herself from snatching her daughter back. Granny wouldn't harm a fly let alone a defenseless baby.

"She'll go far. Look at her eyes, they are the window of the soul. She'll make you proud, Kathleen Green. You and your fancy doctor did well."

Kathleen tried to speak but her voice wouldn't come. Granny had called her by her married name. There was a first time for everything. As she watched, Elsa reached out to Granny's hand and squeezed it in her own. Granny said something.

"What did you say to her?" Kathleen asked.

"It's hard to translate but it means, May you live as long as you want and never want as long as you live." Granny glanced up at Kathleen, her gaze searing a path right into her soul. "What did you think I was doing?"

Kathleen looked away, her cheeks flushing. "I don't understand the Gaelic."

"There's a lot you don't understand. So how are you feeling? You should be watching what you eat. The first three months can be difficult."

Kathleen wondered if the woman had lost her mind. Had she forgotten about the tragedy?

"Granny, I didn't give birth to Elsa. We adopted her after the fire on the boat."

"I know that, you daft eejit. Do you think I lost my mind? I ain't talking about the babe I'm holding but the one you're carryin'."

Kathleen stared at the woman, shock rendering her

speechless. Her legs shook, she grabbed a seat and fell into it. Granny glanced at her before switching her attention back to the baby.

"Elsa, darling girl, you will have to have patience with your mam. She's usually an intelligent woman but sometimes she can act a few sandwiches short of a picnic. So what do you fancy? A brother or a sister? If your mam would make herself useful, we could put on a cup of tea and ask the leaves..."

"No!" Kathleen recovered her strength. " No more magic or tealeaves or anything like that, Granny. I still haven't confessed that sin to Father Nelson."

Granny snorted.

Angry at even thinking the woman could be right, Kathleen tried reasoning with her.

"Granny, what makes you think I'm pregnant? I haven't been sick or anything. There are no signs."

"There are always clues, Kathleen Green, just sometimes we are too blind to see them. Your skin is glowing and your hair looks fuller. You mark my words. You will have your baby by next summer." Granny peered down at Elsa who was now gripping her finger. "You will be a wonderful sister, won't you darling? Yes, you will."

Kathleen sat back in her chair, her hand fluttering over her belly. Could Granny be right? Again?

HISTORICAL NOTE:

The sinking as described in the book happened in real life. I have kept as much of the original details as possible as I hate when people change a real-life event to suit a story.

Mrs. Straub did take her children off the boat after having a premonition something horrible would happen. She was right – almost 750 children died along with over 600 adults.

Mrs. Prawdzichi, the lady Frieda was to help in the story, survived but lost her four daughters. Only her son, Frankie, one of the first children to spot the fire survived.

William Richter, the boy Frieda wanted to meet on the roof, survived as he was working that fateful day. His mother and five siblings died that day. One, ten year old Frances, came home.

Reverend Haas did lose his wife, daughter, sister in

law and nephew in the tragedy and nearly his life as he fought in vain to save his parishioners. His sister, Emma, survived.

Paul Libenow and his wife survived but they lost two of their three daughters. Only their youngest, a baby at the time survived. Paul died six years later in 1910 but by that time had amassed a scrapbook full of every article he found on the disaster.

After the disaster, the area called Little Germany was never the same. Not only had over 1000 of the residents died, but often it was entire families. The only surviving relatives were those who had gone to work that day rather than attending the picnic. Fathers and brothers came home to find their families had died. The rate of suicide amongst those affected rose sharply. Nobody can quantify just how many people were killed by neglect. Because this was no accident. Was it done on purpose? No. Nobody set fire to the boat but due to several people caring more about money than safety, it was a tragedy waiting to happen.

After the horrible event, the church where Reverend Haas preached was seen as a focal point for outpouring of grief. People came in huge numbers to grieve for the victims like the gentle Mary Abend-schein and the members of the band who died.

Frieda and her family aren't real people but those around them were. Frieda and her brother Hans were modeled on some children who did save the lives of others. Few adults never mind children knew how to swim in those days. The real tragedy is that the loss of so many lives was totally preventable. If everyone had done their jobs, the General Slocum would never have been deemed fit for service. The only person who went to jail was the Captain. The rest including the crew members who did nothing to save the passengers, the inspectors who had inspected the boats and lied about their inspections and the owners got off scot free. Why do relatively few people know about this tragedy, especially as it was the greatest loss of life in a single event prior to 9/11? Was it because it was mainly women and children? Or was it the fact they were German? Possibly all of the above. Within ten years of the sinking, Germany was at war and it wasn't seen as a good thing to be German in the USA or Great Britain or most other places outside Germany.

I haven't been able to discover if any orphans traveled the orphan trains as a direct result of losing their parents in the General Slocum tragedy. I imagine some did. The neighbors and friends who may have taken them in, had all either died or suffered horrendous losses themselves. People could no longer face living in Little Germany, and many moved away to Yorkville, Brooklyn or further afield. The repercussions of the tragedy were felt for many years after the event. Unfortunately, with the outbreak of war and the hatred shown towards those from German background, the suffering continued. But mainly in silence.

ALSO BY RACHEL WESSON

Hearts on the Rails

Orphan Train Escape

Orphan Train Trials

Orphan Train Christmas

Orphan Train Tragedy

Printed in Great Britain
by Amazon